Two Roads Diverge

Molly and Jake's Fifteenth Adventure

By Marie and Jerry Perlet

2022

The Road Not Taken

Robert Frost - *1874-1963*

Two roads diverged in a yellow wood,
And sorry I could not travel both
And be one traveler, long I stood
And looked down one as far as I could
To where it bent in the undergrowth;

Then took the other, as just as fair,
And having perhaps the better claim,
Because it was grassy and wanted wear;
Though as for that the passing there
Had worn them really about the same,

And both that morning equally lay
In leaves no step had trodden black.
Oh, I kept the first for another day!
Yet knowing how way leads on to way,
I doubted if I should ever come back.

I shall be telling this with a sigh
Somewhere ages and ages hence:
Two roads diverged in a wood, and I—
I took the one less traveled by,
And that has made all the difference.

Molly and Jake Series

The Reunion Key

Long Lost Friend

On the Trail

The Earworm

The Inti Guard of Machu Picchu

The Artful Deceiver

The President's Confessional

The Just Judges Down Under

Just in Case

Cleopatra's Tomb

The Tahitian Cure

Passageways

Fire and Ice

The Family Tree: Conflicts and Resolutions

<u>Prologue</u>

South Carolina
September, 1860

"Do I hear three? All right. Four? Come, come, gentlemen. These silver candlesticks are the finest in all of South Carolina. Ah, ten. That's more like it." The auctioneer was well-acquainted with the region and pushed prices to their limits. Plus, his commission depended on top dollar for every item sold.

Jeremiah Benjamin Poke was selling his plantation and belongings, all of them. The townspeople thought he was crazy to dispense of such a successful plantation where he could easily become the richest man in the county if he worked it right for another ten years. But . . . he seemed determined to leave South Carolina and no one understood why. The neighboring plantations were quick to purchase the several thousand acres, the equipment, and the slaves. A wealthy state politician purchased the house with a hundred acres around it for his personal residence, his stately palace. The money poured into Jeremiah's accounts as he liquidated absolutely everything.

George Cooper, Jeremiah's closest friend and neighbor, stopped by the next morning as Jeremiah prepared to leave. He wanted to know what had gotten into Jeremiah. Where was he going? What was he thinking?

"I thank you for being a good neighbor and a loyal friend, George. You have been someone I could depend on to have my back. I see a terrible time coming, an unsettling series of events that will disrupt our economy and possibly ruin the South's future. This talk of secession and the foreboding election of Lincoln will lead us to Civil War soon, George. I am moving to Canada until it is all over and I'm taking everything I have with me. You would be wise to do the same. Get out of South Carolina before all hell breaks loose."

"Aw, com'on, Jeremiah. Nobody is going to elect that Lincoln gorilla, and the South is going to rise up and take over the whole country. You'll see. And you'll miss out on all the opportunities to increase your wealth. Good luck to you but I think you are making a huge mistake by running away."

The men shook hands and Jeremiah mounted his horse. He had arranged to have his money converted into gold coins in Charleston; his few family heirlooms and the four chests of gold coins were already loaded onto a ship. He would leave by noon on a voyage to Québec. He wasn't sure about his decision but as he sailed past Fort Sumter, the air just didn't feel right—something terrible was about to happen.

The journey along the Eastern seaboard and then around Newfoundland and into the St. Lawrence River went without incident, a quiet trip lasting about three weeks. Jeremiah had been lucky to find a reputable shipping company owned by a François Beaucour, a wealthy merchant in Québec, to transport his valuables. When the ship docked in Québec, François met him and led him to the local inn. He settled the plantation owner and invited him to dinner at his home near the docks. Jeremiah gladly accepted. His new life had begun and he was thankful he had learned French as a lad. Nobody spoke English here and he would be at a decided disadvantage until he became fluent once again.

Prologue 2

Mandragostan
2018

"Hello, Mr. Beaucour?" The woman's voice was pleasant with a strong Middle Eastern accent. She reminded Jake of Sari Yakim from their Istanbul escapades. "My name is Rabia Begum and I need your help."

Jake recognized the name immediately. Rabia Begum was one of the richest, most influential women in Mandragostan where women were rising to power and wealth under the protection of the United States. *I wonder what she wants?* Jake pondered. "Yes, ma'am. What can I do for you today?"

"Sari Yakim recommended your security company. She said you were the only man she trusted in this world. I am in need of a trained security team that can protect me during these dangerous times in my country. As you are well-aware, women have gained a great deal of power here but are still threatened with repression. Men still try to defy me and put me in my place, threatening to help terrorists kill me. As I have dealt with each one, I have made many enemies. And the United States has indicated that it will be leaving us soon. I need to be surrounded by a team of highly trained, loyal women who will protect me."

Jake discussed the several options that Veritas could provide including personal bodyguards, security systems, monitoring devices, protective clothing, armored limousines, and chauffeur training. Rabia said she wanted a comprehensive plan that outlined all the necessary options and, most importantly, she wanted the trained security team. Jake offered to send two of his top female agents to assess the situation. Rabia knew of Gloria

Lovelace and Sophia Pasternak and she welcomed the opportunity to talk with them.

Gloria had been with Veritas for five years after turning away from her days as a professional scam artist and skilled art forger, now working for the good guys. A computer whiz as well as a strong, gifted woman, Jake respected her tenacity and intelligence. She could teach Rabia the skills of planning and leading a military-style group. Sophia came to Veritas two years ago, her resume extensive. Jake knew she could expertly handle the physical training of the guards. Jake discussed the assignment with Jen and Rich Crockett, the leaders of Veritas, who agreed to the contract. Gloria and Sophia boarded the company jet the next morning with a long list of options to share with Ms. Begum. The trip to Mandragostan was long, over fifteen hours, with a refueling stop in Cairo, giving Gloria and Sophia time to rest and prepare their presentation during the journey.

Following the country's customs, the agents wore slacks, modest blouses, and head scarves as they disembarked in Bulcan. During her life as Rachel Dixon, Gloria had never traveled to Central Africa and knew the region only from her Internet research. Sophia had visited South Africa when she worked for Francesca de la Rondo but knew little about this part of the world. They were met by two of Begum's male assistants and whisked across the city to her estate by a male chauffeur. The men did not speak to the women, effectively communicating their lack of respect for females by ignoring them.

Gloria began observing and recording every security challenge as they approached the estate surrounded by a ten-foot wall outfitted with razor wire. There were four guards at the armored gate brandishing AK-47s, smoking and laughing as the limousine entered the compound. Sophia could already see how these men could turn on a woman in an instant if the money wasn't enough to assure their loyalty. She observed the inexperienced and lack of commitment by the male guards and made a note to discuss the need for trained female guards around Rabia Begum.

The atmosphere changed as Gloria and Sophia were greeted by two professional women in business attire. They were cordial as they led them into the massive house. Gloria scanned every corner for security cameras, observing none. The front door was a standard wooden door and the windows were single-paned glass, all easily breached, bringing about the beginning of a long list of necessary upgrades to the compound.

Sophia observed several female staff working at desks throughout the building; she did not see any men inside the compound. The women were alert, watching the two agents traverse the complex. Gloria thought, *I can see why she wants female security. The discrepancies between the sloths outside and the focused staff inside are stark.* They were ushered into a large sunroom overlooking a well-manicured garden.

A tall, striking young woman, perhaps in her thirties, crossed the room and extended her hand in welcome. Gloria recognized Rabia from pictures in her background files. They shook hands and sat at a large table with a map of the compound. Servers brought tea and a variety of small sandwiches. Gloria smiled. She loved sandwiches, especially these little tea treasures. *Yum.*

"I believe these are your favorites?" Rabia asked as Gloria and Sophia graciously dug into the platter. "And a good beer as well?"

"After we discuss your security, I would love one. Right now, let's take a look at your situation."

Over the next three hours, Gloria and Sophia outlined each area of protection and security. Rabia agreed to all the proposals without hesitation, frequently focusing on defensive training, returning to the issue several times.

She ended the business part of the meeting by stating, "All of this is needed and I will sign all the contracts first thing tomorrow morning. My number one priority, however, is to get twenty women trained so I can replace all the men. The men do a fair job because I pay them very well, but I don't trust them. I want my women around me, trained to handle any situation."

"I can arrange for a Veritas agent to train those you select," Sophia replied.

"I would prefer you do the training yourself. Your reputation as a very effective agent has grown quickly in the past year and I trust you will be able to prepare them now with follow-up during the next few months. Rich and Jen have already agreed to two weeks of intensive training. Sophia, your martial arts abilities are well-known and I hope to learn a great deal from you."

"Well, it depends on how physically fit the women are," Sophia responded. "Security personnel must be extra tough, agile, and sharp. It's a lot more than just being strong and able to shoot a gun."

"Precisely, and that's why I want you to train them. They are already in excellent physical shape and ready to face whatever you throw at them. I will join the training as well so that I, too, am prepared to defeat our enemies. I want them to handle every kind of weapon, especially sniper rifles and grenade launchers." Gloria was surprised to hear of Rabia's' personal interest in the training and her knowledge of weaponry. Her file did indicate that Rabia was trained in self-defense and she was an avid sports enthusiast, mostly in soccer and field hockey; she had been educated at Harvard Business School and had acclimated to many American activities.

Rabia turned to Gloria. "I also understand you are one of Veritas's leading agents in assault planning and strategy. I need a group of five trained in your strategic planning processes so they can lead and organize the others. There will come a time when I will need to plan actions to protect my people and to free hostages. The Bomani are everywhere and we must be ready. I need you to teach us how to do it."

"Again, let me say that this will not happen quickly but we can begin the process of strategic training as well as the physical stuff tomorrow if you like. We will spend this afternoon preparing the equipment and information. Will everyone speak English?"

"Yes. I have insisted that every woman who works for me learn English. We will be ready at nine in the courtyard. My staff will show you to your apartment. Please ask for anything you need. Dinner will be at eight tonight. I hope you can join me."

"Thank you for your hospitality. We'll see you at eight." The staff brought beer to their apartment on a silver tray.

Chapter 1

Present Day
Bryn Mawr

"Jake, it states right here in François' own handwriting: three boxes of gold coins, one thousand jars of honey, and one thousand bottles of Québec rum, lost in the Chesapeake Bay. The captain returned to Québec on horseback to report the ship sinking in the storm. He even described where he thought the boat went down. Look."

Molly handed the journal to Jake and he read the description, studying the hand-drawn map. *"We turned into the bay and we were met by a fierce storm that drove us backwards, into the Atlantic. We fought the storm for more than an hour and suddenly a large floating tree rammed into the side of the ship and we sank within minutes. A few of the sailors reached shore. I was lucky to swim to a hamlet called Moseley's Landing on the Elizabeth River."*

"That's interesting," Molly replied, "because there is no such town on any map of the Chesapeake Bay area. We need to find out where that village was located. And this story about the plantation owner. I'll see what I can dig up on Jeremiah Benjamin Poke. François says he liquidated his South Carolina plantation in 1860 and sailed to Québec with some furniture and four boxes of gold coins. He lived there for ten years. After the Civil War ended and the United States was on the mend, he decided to move back to North Carolina. Apparently, he thought things were better in Raleigh than near Charleston."

"And the worst part for him," Jake pointed out, "was that he was on the ship when it went down and he didn't survive. No family, no one to give anything to. He dies with everything he owned at the bottom of the Chesapeake Bay. That's why we need Mary Lou to investigate this sunken ship and what is still down there."

"I agree. I'll give her a call and we'll get started. I see a trip to the Chesapeake Bay in our future, *monsieur*."

Molly worked all morning to find out where her close friend, Mary Lou Goban, was working. Mary Lou was an archaeologist, always on some adventure. Molly called her 'Indiana Mary'—Mary Lou tolerated the nickname, but only from Molly. After several calls to Mary Lou's university and two museums that she was currently working for, Molly located her in Morocco.

"What on earth could anyone find in Morocco?" she asked Jake. "Isn't it just desert and dust storms there?"

"Oh, you'd be surprised, and I bet Mary Lou is digging up something special. They've found evidence of inhabitants dating back four hundred thousand years. That's like when cavemen were just beginning to get civilized. And the Phoenicians were the first known civilization to colonize the area. So, I'm sure Mary Lou has found some really interesting stuff."

"Okay, well, I think a sunken ship full of gold is pretty 'interesting stuff', too. I'll see if I can get her to come help us on our treasure hunt."

Molly reached Mary Lou who was happy to hear the Beaucours wanted to pursue the sunken ship. Molly had first told her about the ship at Petr and Sophia's wedding, and she had said she would be interested when her current project ended.

"You're in luck. Our work here is almost complete. Probably about two more weeks. I'll send you pictures of what we discovered. Pretty cool stuff. But we're done and the locals can take over and complete the detail work. We need a week to recoup, so how about we meet in Bryn Mawr in three weeks?"

"That's perfect, Mary Lou. When you have your flights, send me the details and we will meet you at the airport."

*   *   *   *   *

When Mary Lou and John arrived, Jake and Molly had their information organized and ready to discuss. The friends spent the afternoon reviewing the journals, the receipts, the maps, and the ancestry research Molly had unearthed about Jeremiah Benjamin Poke. Mary Lou and John formed multiple avenues of inquiry and began outlining the work to be done.

"Jake, don't you have some fancy satellite at Veritas?"

"Well, it doesn't belong to Veritas but we contributed to the cost of the launch and we pay for satellite time whenever we use it. It has really come in handy on some of our cases, especially any involving kidnappings. We can get details on very specific locations including live video and heat signatures."

"Can it penetrate the ground or water?"

"Yes, it can. I believe we used it in Peru when we were searching for the Incan ruins."

"Right, I remember that. Can we use it to survey the Chesapeake Bay?"

"We can try. I'll contact the satellite team and find out. We're looking for a ship that is probably rotted away, but the cargo included a thousand bottles of Canadian rum, a thousand jars of honey, and three chests of gold coins. Right?"

"Yes," Molly replied. "According to François' journal, Jeremiah was returning to the United States with his three boxes of gold coins and large quantities of products he was producing in Canada, rum and honey. Jeremiah went down with the ship, and there were no descendants."

"Mary Lou, according to maritime law, who will own whatever we find?"

"This is very complicated," John replied. "We will no doubt need lawyers to deal with all the red tape. Basically, if the ship went down in international waters, at least twelve miles from the U.S. coastline, then it belongs to whoever finds it and brings it up. But if the ship is in U.S. and Maryland or Virginia waters, the issue must be negotiated with the states and the feds."

"Hmmm, any chance the ship was driven that far out into the open ocean?" Molly asked.

"Time will tell. The area we are looking at is huge. We need to narrow down the search, so we must first find this Moseley's Landing on the Elizabeth River. We know where the river is, so where is this town?"

They studied the Bay maps trying to locate the mysterious Moseley's Landing and were not having much luck until John searched the Internet for Moseley in Virginia, revealing a family line in the Virginia Beach area. "That looks promising since Virginia Beach is in the area we are exploring," John explained.

Jake left to call Veritas and get the information about the satellite. Molly decided to let the Gobans work on the Moseley issue so she could continue to learn more about Jeremiah Poke. By dinnertime, the pieces of the puzzle began to fall into place.

"You always have such delicious and unique dishes, Molly. This moussaka is perfect, as good as any I have had in Greece. And I always love the cottage cheese on the salad. It reminds me of my mom's dinners. Thank you so much for welcoming us into your home once again."

"We enjoy our adventures with you," Jake replied. "You guys always have the most unique treasure hunts."

"Well, thank you, Jake. This trip to Morocco was something else. We were unearthing an early Phoenician trading settlement and we stumbled upon a large collection of glass bottles and bowls. The Phoenicians discovered the art of glass blowing and this collection belonged to a rich nobleman who lived in the villa we were excavating.

"The Phoenicians invented many of our modern conveniences. They created our alphabet based on phonetic sounds rather than symbols and pictures, and their craftsmen discovered how to make a rich purple dye from mollusk shells that the Roman emperor declared his personal royal color, hence the term 'royal purple.' The Phoenician mariners sailed the seas and even rounded the Cape of Good Hope, devising many sailing techniques including navigating by the stars. And their glassblowing was a nobleman's luxury throughout the Mediterranean region. Quite a prolific civilization."

"I guess so," Molly said. "Wow, I didn't know all of that. Interesting what we have learned from early civilizations. Now, on our current project, I confirmed that Poke did not have any descendants and no recorded will. Any issue involving ownership of the treasure will have to go through Maryland, Virginia, or the United States."

"Unless the ship is in international waters and then it's finders-keepers," John reminded the group.

"Good," Mary Lou continued. "If we succeed in finding the site that will help a lot. John and I studied several colonial maps of the Elizabeth River and we found Mosely's Landing. It was located on the banks of the Elizabeth, in the present-day area of Lambert's Point at the mouth of the river. The ship's captain must have washed ashore and someone found him. It was a miracle he made it to shore.

"Our next step will be to learn about the currents in this area and the prevailing directions of most storms. The captain's journal says the ship fought the storm for more than an hour before sinking. John and I will spend the next week at our lab developing a simulation of the ship's size and weight, and the currents and prevailing winds at the mouth of the Chesapeake. That should help us narrow the search area."

"And I talked with the satellite techs," Jake shared. "They have not used the satellite on ocean searches before, so they are going to study a known shipwreck off the Carolina coast to see what they can do with the technology. They can't promise it will work but they are very hopeful."

"Great, then we have some next steps to get underway. We'll develop the simulation, you explore the satellite, and Molly, can you arrange some warehouse space in Norfolk. I'll send you a list of the supplies that we will need including a boat."

The dessert of chocolate crepes and homemade vanilla ice cream was scrumptious as they discussed their previous adventures. Mary Lou was already planning her next trip to Newgrange in Ireland, an ancient monument similar to the famous Stonehenge. She had stumbled across some clues to the origin and the meaning of the monument and wanted to explore the region further. Molly said it sounded like a mysterious and fun trip. Maybe they could go along? *Hint, hint.*

Chapter 2

Present Day
Veritas

Gloria and Sophia were carefully monitoring the developing situation in Mandragostan through Veritas surveillance and the news media. They had maintained contact with Rabia Begum since 2018 and visited once a year to check her security setup. They were certain Rabia would have the means and the good sense to escape the country before her estate was overrun by the invading Bomani.

The United States withdrawal of military support was expected but the sudden reduction of U.S. forces without much preparation had taken the Mandragonians by surprise. The Bomani were quickly taking control of everything. The expectation that the Bomani would control the country in a matter of days was shocking. Mandragostan would suffer the loss of the freedoms of women, children, and the elderly as well as the economic prowess that had grown over the past ten years—a national disaster.

Gloria knew Rabia's history. She was born into a rich merchant's family and raised in a typical submissive fashion to men. Her servant girl was her playmate in her early years and she saw how the child was mistreated, even raped by an elder relative, and treated like an animal or a piece of property. The little girl did not go to school and was often beaten. Rabia was not going to grow up as anyone's slave and constantly questioned the position of women in Mandragostan. As the child of a wealthy Mandragonian, she was educated at home by tutors and her father, a more liberal Muslim, protected her from abuse and taught her about his business. When the time came, he willingly sent her to the United States for a proper college education. She excelled at the small women's college graduating first in her class. It was no surprise that Harvard eagerly accepted her into their school of business. By the time she graduated, Mandragostan had become more open to women in business and she returned to take over her father's large import/export business. He was ill and then died, leaving full control of the company to his Harvard-educated daughter.

The company expanded rapidly under her guidance, taking full advantage of the influx of money from the United States occupation. When Gloria and Sophia met her in 2018, Rabia was the wealthiest woman in Mandragostan, wielding economic power over many men. She had been correct about jealous men wanting to harm her. There had been three attempts on her life in three years, all ending with piles of male corpses at her gate. The estate was like a fortress, even sustaining a bombing attack. The Veritas training was protecting her interests.

Sophia reminded Gloria of the three practice scenarios they had used in their training and how eerily prophetic they were. The first practice was a direct assault on the compound. Sophia organized a Veritas team of eight to attack and Rabia's security team responded. Using paint guns for the practice, Rabia's team "killed" all eight agents within five minutes. Sophia was surprised.

The second practice run was an attack on Rabia's limousine. Sophia's team used firecrackers to simulate bombs, "blowing up" the first car in the caravan, and then attacking Rabia's limousine. The third car of Rabia's security team and a separate back-up car of her people annihilated Sophia's team in no time.

The third practice was a hostage situation in the compound. Sophia's team took Rabia hostage. Rabia was a very effective hostage using psychological probes to distract her captors. Her security people infiltrated the compound and "killed" all the kidnappers without any harm to Rabia. The security team was incredibly efficient at protecting Rabia Begum.

Gloria reminded Sophia of their dinner the last night at the compound. Rabia was most appreciative of all they had done and gave them extravagant gifts. She also told stories of women who had grasped power and used it for good. She was fighting for them. There was Garhawshad Begum, a distant relative and a renowned political figure during the Timurid dynasty (1370-1507) in Afghanistan. Then Rabia Balkhi, a famous poet in the ninth century, declaring her love for a man who was not approved by her elders. Queen Soraya Tarzi promoted women's rights and education for all during her husband's rule, 1919 to 1929.

Rabia had studied the lives of Emmeline Pankhurst and her daughters, and Susan B. Anthony and Elizabeth Cady Stanton, all women who sacrificed their comfortable lives to get the vote for women. She learned about Madame Curie and other famous women scientists who had stood their ground demanding their research be acknowledged. And Colonel Malalai Kakar, a personal friend of Rabia's, head of the Afghanistan Department of Crimes Against Women, assassinated by a Taliban gunman in 2008. Kakar became the model heroine for Rabia's security team.

Rabia was also close to Sari Yakim, another wealthy woman who had dominated her business in Istanbul and would not bend to men. They would meet often to console and support each other and plan their next steps in business and their personal lives. Sari was another Veritas client.

Gloria and Sophia were very pleased that their training had produced such great results. When they had started, they were surprised by the strength and agility of the Mandragostan women. They were smart and learned quickly, eagerly seeking any knowledge of hand-to-hand combat and the use of weapons. Gloria had trained five of the women in strategic planning and they were applying it every day in their security protocols.

What the two Veritas agents did not know was that Rabia had used the training and strategic planning to build a secret army, hidden away in the hills around Bulcan. She had recruited a thousand women who had lived in three compounds deep in the mountains for the past three years. The women trained daily in all forms of defensive moves, skilled at weaponry, hand-to-hand combat, and small-group interventions. While Gloria thought a small security team defended Rabia's estate, in reality each assault on the compound had been met by a large group of highly trained women who showed no mercy to their enemies. Every single man who attacked was brutally slaughtered to set an example to anyone who would threaten Rabia Begum. Men learned to respect her security team.

As the Bomani swarmed across Mandragostan and the United States withdrew, Rabia understood what was coming. The Bomani would never let women like her continue holding positions of power, politically or economically. They would target her and overrun her compound. All the progress in educating young women and freeing them from the suppression of a male-dominated society would be lost. She took steps to prepare for the invasion.

All her assets were secure in accounts outside of Mandragostan. While she would lose her estate, her vast fortune was safe. She moved everyone from the compound to one of the camps in the mountains and prepared her army. The Bomani would be in for a big surprise when the time was appropriate. She assured Gloria and Sophia that she was taking steps to leave Mandragostan. Not knowing about the secret army, they were relieved to hear this and offered to help Rabia in any way.

Chapter 3

Present Day
Norfolk, Virginia

Molly had secured a new warehouse on the Norfolk waterfront. Mary Lou and John were very pleased with the facility and its location. The new boat was large enough to sail out into the ocean with sonar and other exploration equipment, and there was a large flat deck to spread out any salvaged material. They set up their lab inside the warehouse awaiting the arrival of the Beaucours the following week.

Mary Lou and John performed their computer simulation of the Chesapeake Bay region more than fifty times, changing parameters to see where the ship might have sunk. They mapped an area of approximately one hundred square miles, a large search area that would take some time to scan with sonar. They would begin the search in the deeper ocean and work toward the coastline.

The Gobans provided their search area to the Veritas satellite team and were awaiting the photographs of the area. Veritas had conferred with another archaeologist who used satellite imagery for her explorations. No one was sure the satellite would be able to penetrate the water deep enough but it would significantly cut down their exploration time if they could locate shipwrecks with the satellite technology.

Jake and Molly arrived in Norfolk on Monday morning with big smiles and several large photographs of the Goban's search area. "We may have too many sites to explore," Jake said. "The satellite team found seventeen potential wrecks. They know that six of the wrecks are identified and documented, leaving the other eleven for speculation and exploration. Here you go." Jake spread the photos on the table.

All four spent the morning studying each image with magnifying glasses, making notes about each shape, size, position, distance from Norfolk, and depth. They were able to narrow the possibilities down to four. The other seven wrecks had definitive sizes and shapes that showed them to be modern, metal, power-driven, even possibly military ships.

"Good work, guys," John commented. "Now let's study these four. First, notice that these two are on the edge of our search area; the ship might have drifted this far depending on the storm, but our model would suggest these are outliers. The other two fall more in the center.

"And the depth of the first one is easily accessible with our robot sub. We can do a preliminary exploration of this one in one day. The other one is about twice as deep with stronger currents and will take a bit longer. I would say we start with these two and see what we find. Then try three and four."

Everyone followed John's logic and agreed. They would begin tomorrow.

*　　*　　*　　*　　*

Mary Lou had hired two local fishermen to navigate the boat. The two couples would be the remainder of the crew handling the equipment. John was usually in charge of the actual exploration and he was an expert at steering the minisub through all kinds of ocean terrain and currents. The fishermen used Mary Lou's coordinates to steer the boat to the first location and John dropped a sonar detector over the side to begin preliminary searches.

Everyone studied the screens for a response to the pings as the fishermen sailed the boat back and forth in a pattern over the search area. It took most of the morning for the sonar to locate the potential wreck. Mary Lou marked the exact GPS location. She asked the fishermen to maintain their location while the four readied the minisub and sent it down into the murky water.

"We're going to use infrared cameras on this first dive since there is so much mud in the water. Once we locate the wreck we can switch to the visual cameras and see what we have."

The minisub slowly descended to the bottom, the motors specifically designed to prevent too much stirring of the mud. John maneuvered the sub carefully to the spot. Images began to appear on the screen.

"*Oooo*, look at that," Molly exclaimed. "That looks like something out of a Scooby Doo cartoon, a pirate wreck on the ocean floor. How exciting."

"Scooby Doo? You're spending too much time with the grandkids, Molly-O," Jake chuckled.

"But she's right, Jake. Look at the curve of the wooden bow. A lot has rotted away, but you can see the outline of the ship. This could be a pirate ship or the one we are looking for. Definitely wooden, about the correct size and shape. Let's take a closer look."

John switched to the visual cameras and moved the sub around the wreck, video recording all the observations. Mary Lou studied each angle, pointing at several parts of the ship. As John rounded the back of the vessel, she caught a glimpse of a nameplate.

"Check that out, John. Zoom in on it."

As the name came into view, all four groaned. "The Golden Flounder? Who would name a ship that? Do you think it's a joke?"

"Got it," said Mary Lou as she searched the web for The Golden Flounder. She turned the screen so everyone could see it. "It's a replica of an old sailing ship, used for tourists out of Norfolk. It sank in a hurricane about twelve years ago. Satellite images and sonar were right about the shape of an old ship, but it's not ours. She made a note on the map about the GPS coordinates and the name. There might be a finder's fee if they reported it to the company.

"Well, first day was a bust. Let's head back to port and get some rest. Tomorrow, we go after number two."

"Are we outside the twelve-mile limit?"

"No, unfortunately. Both of these sites are only ten miles from the shore. The other two are in deeper water but definitely at least fifteen miles from land. Number two is the most obvious one for our ship. Let's see what we find."

After a relaxing dinner at Sally's Crab Shack, the couples collapsed into their respective beds. Dreams of shipwrecks, storms at sea, and chests of treasures danced through their heads all night.

The next morning the sailors were prepared for the second attempt. The procedures were the same and the sonar located the second wreck by midmorning. By noon the minisub was descending into deeper and more turbulent waters. John steered the sub down toward the dark sea bottom.

"We're luckier here since the water is clearer. It is very dark, though, so we will use high-powered lights." John flipped a switch and suddenly they could see the ocean bottom. A large fish swam across the camera lens.

"*Whoa!* That was a big one," one of the fishermen exclaimed at the doorway. "We'll be coming back here with our fishing boat."

"Good idea," Jake laughed.

Mary Lou laid her hand on Jake's and waited for the fisherman to head back to the wheel. "We'll talk later, but we will need to be careful what we share with these guys. Too many treasures have been lost to the crews who listen and return during the night and steal it before the treasure hunters return the next day to retrieve what they find. Some admiral said…"

Jake smiled, "Loose lips sink ships. Often used in World War II to remind sailors to keep the ship's location a secret so German subs wouldn't sink them. My lips are sealed."

Molly nodded her head in agreement. She would be careful in her friendly talk with the fishermen to not mention what they were really looking for.

"Will you look at that," John pointed to the screen. "That ship is in pretty good condition. I guess the colder water has preserved it, but the currents have buried about half the ship in silt. Let's see what we can find."

John conducted a search similar to the first ship, moving along the bow to the stern, searching for any clues. Mary Lou watched anxiously. "There. Zoom in on that." She pointed to an object that looked like a bell. John focused two spotlights on the object and slowly zoomed the lens. The image became clearer.

"Ships of this era used bells like foghorns. When they were sailing in the mist, one of the crew would ring the bell every minute to alert other ships. That's a good sign. Let's look for more clues."

John recorded over two hours of video, zooming in on several objects. The ship did not have a nameplate, but there were several crates in the hold that were promising. He needed to use special visual processing programs back at the warehouse to study the crates more closely. By late afternoon, they had collected as much data as they could, and would discuss next steps during the evening to decide on tomorrow's tasks. Mary Lou recorded the GPS location on her map and labeled it "Number 2."

That night, Mary Lou asked Molly to invent a scenario for their explorations. "These fishermen were very interested in our location today. They're smart and they probably already know we are searching for a vessel, and they are noting locations on their instruments. So, we need a story about a sunken ship and what we are looking for. I know you can make it believable."

Molly laughed. "We could really throw them and say we are looking for an alien spaceship."

"Believable, Molly," Mary Lou chuckled. "These guys aren't gullible. They would probably sell that story to the press and then we would have a major mess on our hands."

"Okay, I get it. I'll have it ready for breakfast tomorrow."

*　　*　　*　　*　　*

Molly read her background story while eating scrambled eggs, and John shared what he had found in his photos.

"Once I had the photos loaded into the computer, I could study that bell more closely. There was a date on the rim, 1879. Unfortunately, this is not our ship. It could have promising cargo to explore since the crates still had very faintly painted labels about glassware and Jamestown. Mary Lou and I will put this on our future list, but we won't waste any more time on this one. We need to move on to ship three."

"So, here is what we are really doing," Molly began. "We are searching for the ship on which Jake's great grandfather sailed to reach the new world in the early 1800s. That's sort of true so it will be easy to talk about. Jake wants to find the ship for his sentimental ancestry research. We don't have to mention any cargo, just the ship."

"That works for me," Mary Lou replied. "Let's head out for number three."

Farther out in the ocean, it took about three hours to reach the site. The water was deeper and John had to drop the sonar much lower and take more time with the readings. Eventually they found the signature at noon and sent the sub down.

"Ma'am, weather station is reporting a storm moving in around five. We will need to head back in an hour."

"Okay, Captain. Thanks for the info. We're just going to do a preliminary scan with the sub and then we'll be ready to go."

John moved as quickly as he could, reached the wreck and began the visual scan. After an hour, Mary Lou told him to pack it in as the sky now looked threatening and dark. They reached the Norfolk docks just as the front swept through the area, drenching everyone on board.

*   *   *   *   *

"The captain says the seas are too rough today, so we have a day to rest and review the situation. I've got something really interesting in the video I want to show you."

After a hearty breakfast, they moved to the warehouse to see what John had found. "First, the shape and size are correct for a sailing ship of the mid-nineteenth century. Second, the damage to the deck area is consistent with a storm. Notice the broken railings and the snapped off mast. The ship was heavily damaged before it sank.

"We are fortunate that the layer of silt is not too thick since the currents have kept the ship fairly clean of settling dirt. The very cold water has also worked to our favor, preserving the wood. Now, notice this."

The camera focused down the side of the ship detecting a large hole in the bow. "This is consistent with a puncture, presumably the tree trunk, which would have caused the ship to sink quickly. I did not have enough time to reach the rear of the ship, so no name to check but the last thing in the video is another bell. I made a still photo of the bell and zoomed in on the rim where the date is recorded, 1851. That's right in the middle of the timeframe we are looking for."

"*Wow!* This is all very promising," Jake said. "I have many questions."

Mary Lou smiled. "Just a maybe, Jake. Maybe. We need to finish the video survey before we make any further decisions."

"Okay, but just let's say we found the ship. What are the next steps?"

The treasure hunters spent the morning discussing what they would do once they were sure they had found the right ship, and then they reviewed the video and sonar reports again. Before lunch, John called the boat captain who said the weather reports were favorable for the next day—they would make the final decision in the morning.

"Looks like we can't do much more today," John reported back to the group. "I'll use this afternoon to prepare equipment for tomorrow."

"I have to finish up some reports on our Morocco exploration, so I'll settle in our hotel room and get that done."

“Molly and I will go on a land exploration and check out the area around the mystical Moseley's Landing. See you guys for dinner around seven.”

Chapter 4

Bryn Mawr

"Hey, Gloria! Are we still on for this weekend in New York City?" Noah sounded very excited and friendly, that voice of his so smooth and charming.

Gloria responded in kind. "Oh yes, Noah. I am really looking forward to it. I bought tickets to one of the Broadway shows. I hope that was okay."

"Great! I love musicals. And I booked us a suite with two bedrooms at a hotel near Penn Station. I figured that would be an easy trip for you from Philly."

"Terrific! I'll see you there on Friday around five?"

"See you then."

Busy monitoring developments in Mandragostan, Gloria and Sophia hoped for some word on where Rabia was hiding. They would need to visit her to re-establish security at her new location. So far, no new information, so they headed home for dinner.

Their living arrangement was very satisfying. As a part of their contracts, Veritas provided a four-bedroom house on the Veritas campus that they shared, enjoying their close friendship while maintaining their own private spaces within the dwelling. Newly married, Sophia spent the work week at Veritas in Bryn Mawr and then flew to Boston for weekends with Petr near his lab, and sometimes Petr visited Bryn Mawr.

Gloria tended to be a private person, enjoying living with Sophia, going out with other women friends once in a while, and most weekends retreating into her own world of gaming competitions online. "Copycat" was her screen name and she was known on many platforms as a fierce competitor and most of the time a top winner.

This coming weekend Petr was coming to Bryn Mawr and Gloria was traveling outside of her comfort zone, heading to New York City for a rendezvous with Noah Chambers. They had met at Sophia's wedding three months prior and it seemed to be love at first sight for them both. But—they were going slow to be sure. Gloria continued to struggle with her mixed feelings about Noah and she finally shared her feelings with Sophia at dinner. Sophia was an excellent listener and had experience with several Italian men and Petr. She could help Gloria sort out these conflicting emotions.

"I need your advice on this weekend jaunt to New York."

"Okay, what's up?"

"You know I met Noah at your wedding, only that wasn't the first time I met him."

"Really?"

"In my former life, I used him as a fence for two Rembrandts that I stole. That was ten years ago in Paris, another face and hair color and name. I don't think he knows who I really am. What I know is that he was a crook back then, and I think he is still in the game."

"Gosh, Petr thinks so highly of him. He was his best man."

"Well, Noah has done a really good job of keeping his identity secret. Interpol doesn't even know who they are looking for, just a gentleman thief. Their nickname for him is Sir Hood, a reference to Robin Hood. He's still a thief even if he does it with finesse."

"*Hmmm*, tough to be on the right side of the law and fall for a guy who is on the wrong side."

"Well, that's the thing. I have never felt this way about any man. In all my relationships with men I have always been in charge. I have decided what would happen when, and when everything would end. There has never been a commitment from me and I guess you could say I was using those men. But now, there is something very magnetic about our relationship, a very different feeling, and I keep wondering if Noah is the one guy I am meant to be with. I am willing to let him lead some of the time."

"So, you do have feelings for him."

"Oh yeah, I'm falling pretty hard with dreams and fantasies and all that emotional stuff I never do. So, my dilemma is weird. Do I let myself fall in love with a guy I know is a thief? Do I tell him how I really know him? Do I ask him to stop being a thief and change his ways for me? Am I just hoping he might change? The thinking goes on and on and I feel like I'm going insane!"

"The one thing I don't want to do," Sophia stated, "is having to chase you all over the world if you go back to your Rachel self, so I hope that is not on the table."

"And that's the one thing I know for certain. I am not going back. Jake and Molly gave me one chance to do things right and I want to stay on that track. No guy, even if I love him so deeply, is going to lead me away from that commitment. If it comes down to a choice, I know the final answer."

"Then everything else that can happen," Sophia pondered, "hinges on that foundation. How about this? You're an investigator, so you investigated him and found out he is not an investor, but a master thief. Tell him outright that you know. As long as he doesn't involve you in his business, you don't plan to tell anyone about it. You can see me as your insurance, the only other person who knows."

"And what is he going to say?"

"You're smart, you're clever. You will need to weigh his response. Maybe he wants to come clean, so we can devise some way to redeem him, the way Molly and Jake have treated us. Maybe he says he wants to continue to be a thief, so you end it, friendly and polite and all, but you tell him this relationship will not work out. Your heart will break and I'll be here for you, but you know you can't have it both ways. Gloria, I know you well enough that I know you cannot live that double life."

"It's already driving me crazy. What if this guy has robbed a Veritas client? I should be turning him in."

"Unfortunately, there is a third possibility in this relationship. He could be playing you to get information on clients for future crimes, using you by pretending to love you."

"That would suck. I won't let that happen."

"For your own sake, keep me in the loop."

"That's what partners are for."

They moved on to other topics, enjoyed their pasta and sauce, and finished the evening with a good action movie. It was funny for two real secret agents to watch the Hollywood version of their work. "I think we are superheroes."

Sophia headed to bed and Gloria prepared for her trip to NYC. She would leave on the three o'clock train from Philly after a morning shift at Veritas.

*　　*　　*　　*　　*

There he was, standing with a bouquet of red roses, smiling at her as she ascended the stairs from the train station. It was a really nice surprise and she could feel that "love him" side shouting in her head while the cautious side whispered "be careful." She kissed him anyway and the long embrace felt so, so good.

They walked hand-in-hand down the street to a brand new, very modern hotel, Noah carrying her overnight bag and Gloria clutching her bouquet of roses. This felt good, it felt right, could she make this work? They checked in, splitting the bill on two credit cards, and they flew in the elevator to the fourteenth floor. Suite 1407 was beautiful with a sitting room, two bedrooms, two baths, and a mini-kitchen. The view was spectacular, a large picture window framing the Empire State Building.

"Hmmm, Sleepless in Seattle tonight?" Noah asked.

Gloria poked him in the ribs. "I'm planning on getting a good night's sleep, but yeah, I like that movie. Tom Hanks is sweet and Meg Ryan's character is familiar."

"When is our Broadway show?"

"Tomorrow night at seven. Let's find some dinner and then watch the movie. I'm really hungry."

They wandered up Broadway to Times Square and found Ellen's Stardust Diner right in the middle of all the action, one of Noah's favorite NYC diners. The food was great deli, and the wait staff were actors and singers who wanted to be on Broadway— they literally sang, danced, and acted for their supper. Gloria had never seen anything like it and they had an exhilarating time singing along and cheering the actors on. After a leisurely stroll back to the hotel, followed by the movie on the big screen TV in the sitting room, the lights of the city and the Empire State Building glowing in the distance, they snuggled together under a blanket. As the credits rolled, the mood became very romantic.

"I have to tell you that I am really smitten by you, Gloria. I know it sounds corny but I have never met a woman quite like you and I am mesmerized by your beauty, your brains, and your guts. I'm not sure where this relationship will end up, though I hope we can always be friends even if we're not lovers."

Gloria could feel the blush on her face. Thank goodness it was dark in the room. "I have to admit that I have had those strange feelings since the wedding, something so different from other guys I've met. It doesn't matter to me that you are wealthy and successful. I am just looking for someone I can trust and enjoy life with, in a shack or a mansion, rich or poor, just honesty and friendship." She knew she was falling in love and she also was planting the necessary expectation up front—honesty. She wondered where that might go and watched his eyes.

"I couldn't agree more," Noah said as he sat up and faced her. "I would guess as a secret agent you've done your homework on me."

Gloria looked into his eyes. "Yeah, actually I have. I have to say that someone has created an excellent cover for your work."

Noah stared into her eyes with a frown on his forehead. "Not sure what you mean."

"Let's say 'international investor' is a kind way to describe what you really do, Sir Hood."

He gasped and slid back on the couch. "Are you really that good?"

"Yes, I am. In my line of work, I am an expert techie. I am one of the best hackers in the world. It's hard to keep secrets from me. Your dark website gave you away."

Noah bowed his head and stared at the carpet. "That would mean that if I bothered one of your clients, you would be on the hunt for me."

"Yep, that would be right. You haven't, have you?" Noah shook his head. They sat for a few moments in silence, each calculating their next move.

Gloria took a deep breath and said, "Would you ever consider going straight, giving it up? Don't you have enough money that you really don't need to continue?" She was going for it all now. Would he think about changing?

"That would take some real soul searching, Gloria. You know how you get used to doing something, it becomes a habit, a way of living every day. Just stopping would be difficult. It's like an addiction, the rush of outsmarting some rich person."

"Interpol calls you 'Sir Hood' because they think you are robbing from the rich and giving to the poor? Does that really happen?"

"Sorry, no, it's part of the storyline. I haven't shared much with anyone other than the standard charity donations any wealthy person would make. I have thought about giving up the whole gig before but I have a bigger problem. So, you know the whole story, two years ago I took a job for Herr Donovan, an affluent German who wanted a jeweled crown from a small museum in Naples. The caper was pretty simple and I easily extracted the crown and delivered the goods. Only, instead of handing me a check for services rendered, he handed me a copy of a museum security video that clearly showed my face as I picked up the crown. He had set the whole thing up to blackmail me into his service.

"I do my own thing most of the time, but he is a regular customer who I can't say no to. Even if I wanted to stop, he would turn me over to Interpol in an instant and you know the end of that story. What I do for him is not noble, nor is it for the poor, only for his greed and my freedom from prison."

Gloria thought they had breached the subject and they both needed time to think about the situation. She could also glean that Noah was not jumping at the idea of going straight. That set off her alarm bells.

"Well, we have the room for the weekend. We might as well take advantage of it," she pointed out. "Let's put this topic aside and think about it some more later, compartmentalize it. Can you do that?" Noah nodded and smiled. "I want to enjoy this weekend, together. The movie was nice, but I'm not sure what would make me sleepless in this city." Gloria smiled and winked at Noah.

Noah grinned. "Your room or mine?"

Gloria was not sure where this would end up, but for the next two days and nights, she was going to concentrate on enjoying this man. After a few hours in bed, the couple ventured out into the city that never sleeps to find some late-night dessert.

*　*　*　*　*

In the middle of the night with her back pressed up against Noah's chest, she thought about the conversation. She was asking him to be honest, no secrets. How could she keep Rachel a secret from him? She had decided to tell him about her previous life, but then she thought more about it when he started talking about blackmail. If he was still in the business, determined to set up a new crime, he could use that information to blackmail her. She wasn't going there. Rachel Dixon would remain dead and buried. Hilda Berkheimer had told her that she had lived with her secret identity for more than fifty years, had let dead dogs lie. Gloria could do that, too.

Noah woke up, nestled against Gloria's back. This felt so good, so real, so permanent. Maybe he could go straight to be with this woman. But he wasn't going to prison, and Herr Donovan would send him there for a long time. As much as he would enjoy life with Gloria, it was just too dangerous. No, he had to stick to his game plan. Maybe a box of gold coins could buy the video from Donovan. Maybe he could break free from the German. They could enjoy each other's company until Gloria found out what he was really up to, then he would be on the run from her. That would be very hard but he could not think of another choice.

Chapter 5

Norfolk

As they boarded the boat the next morning, Molly reported on their exploration of the surrounding neighborhood. Nobody they talked to had ever heard of Moseley's Landing, but the Beaucours did find some dusty old records in the town hall that included information about the colonial village. Nothing about any shipwrecks.

The captain stopped by the cabin and asked for the GPS coordinates. Mary Lou shared them, a bit suspicious that he didn't already have the information. Maybe this was a ruse to cover up any intentions the fishermen had of stealing whatever they found. An hour out into the ocean, the captain came back to the cabin.

"I know you are searching for something, and your talk of a shipwreck suggests you are looking for treasure. I have dealt with treasure hunters before and you should know that I will not break any laws to keep whatever you find a secret, no matter how much you offer to pay me. If you are planning anything illegal then this should be our last trip out here together."

"I do appreciate your honesty, Captain," Jake replied. "We are well aware of the laws involved and would contact the authorities if we found anything within the water boundaries of Virginia or Maryland. We are searching for a ship that my great grandfather sailed from Québec, a trading vessel. This is an ancestor-thing, finding something of my grandfather's. Are we outside the twelve-mile limit?"

"Yes, if this is where you are looking, we are almost twenty miles from the coast. But you will need to prove ownership to avoid any trouble."

"If we locate the ship that sank over one hundred and fifty years ago, and that is a big if, we will establish ownership of the vessel and anything we find. Again, I thank you for being up-front and for your advice, and I assure you that we do not intend on breaking any laws. We'll let you know."

"Interesting conversation," John reflected as the captain departed. "Everything you said was true and his approach was interesting as well, stating he wouldn't take a bribe."

"Eyes open everybody," Mary Lou chimed in. "I hope he is an honest man, but I have dealt with many who lose that honesty when gold is involved."

When the boat reached the site, John lowered the mini-sub for another look around. He located the wreck and maneuvered the cameras to the rear. The name of the ship was still painted across the back, the *Lady Sophie*. "Bingo, guys, we hit pay dirt!" Molly exclaimed. "That's the ship in the journal, and François' wife's name. This is it!"

John continued to survey the ship, noting places where divers or equipment could enter the hold. Because of the depth, this would require some additional equipment, which would delay the dive by a day. He did his best to maneuver the sub near the hole in the side, shining a bright light into the dark but the camera didn't pick up anything. Tomorrow would be an adventure right out of National Geographic—John and two other divers would explore the ship.

As they headed back to port, the captain asked, "Is this it?"

"It is a strong possibility but until we get some divers down there tomorrow, we won't know for certain. The wreck is the right size and the location is pretty accurate. We will be looking for clues that would identify the ship as my grandfather's and then go from there. We may have to move on to the fourth location."

*   *   *   *   *

Each diver sported a video camera on his forehead and an earpiece and mic for communication between the surface and each other. The murky sea cleared as they descended deeper, and the current was strong but manageable. It took about twenty minutes to reach the wreck.

The number one objective was to locate the cargo. Mapping the site would come later as well as documentation of the discovery, important steps for Mary Lou and John. While much was already known about ships of this era, additional finds were always welcomed by maritime historians.

The gaping hole in the bow of the ship was the logical entryway. Using strong searchlights, the three entered the hold. One of the dangers in exploring sunken vessels was the collapse of the inner parts of the ship. If a diver accidentally bumped into a post, everything could come crashing down. If a school of fish or other animals was disturbed and caused a sudden whoosh of current, that could disrupt delicate balances. So, they proceeded one at a time, cautiously moving into the ship, tethered together by a rope, fifty feet apart.

"This is amazing considering how long this has been down here. Under this layer of silt, the cargo is still in crates. Can you see them in the video?"

"Yes," Mary Lou answered. "I'm saving still photos of each crate to see if we can find the labels. Jake, Molly, use that monitor to start looking at each one."

The Beaucours reviewed each picture for clues. On the third photo, Jake pointed at the screen. "This one . . . right here . . . it says JB Poke. Also, the word 'miel', French for honey."

The divers slowly backed up to the crate. John grasped the box to see if it was sturdy. Pieces of wood crumbled under his gloves, but he could see the contents. He pulled out a jar. "Well, lookie here, French honey. Let's check out some of these others. Get photos first and then open them up. Each diver carefully photographed piles of crates, one at a time, and then began opening them.

"More honey over here, sir."

"Honey here, too."

"Mine are honey, too," John said. "We need to move on to the next group of crates."

They placed the jars of honey into a basket and then carefully swam into the next section of the hull. Jake used the crane to bring the basket to the surface, unloading the honey jars into a crate on the deck.

A startled baby shark swam out the open hatch in the deck above the swimmers. Little flakes of wood sifted down through the water. "Let's check these crates."

Each diver looked at another pile of crates, photographing them, and then opening them. Written on the labels: JB Poke and 'rhum'.

"Sir, these are bottles of rum, and they look like they might be good enough to drink!"

"Mine, too. Probably twenty-five bottles in each crate. That's a lot of bottles, John."

Mary Lou, Jake, and Molly stared at the screen. The whole story was unfolding before them—honey, rum, and . . .?

John spoke softly as he swam to another area in the hull, while the other divers put the rum bottles in the basket. "Here they are, three crates with chests inside. The chests are padlocked shut, so I can't open them here. We will need heavier equipment to get them to the surface. We have just about used up our time for this dive, so we are coming up. We'll plan our next steps for tomorrow."

Mary Lou cranked the basket up to the surface, unloading the bottles of rum. Jake filmed the basket as it came out of the water. The captain stood and watched.

"Have we found what we came looking for?" he asked.

"We have found the ship," Jake replied. "According to my grandfather's log, it was filled with rum and honey. Looks like we found what we were looking for."

The captain smiled and asked to see the bottle of rum. "I wonder if it is any good."

Molly carefully took the bottle from the captain, grinning. "Time to find out. Do you have something to open it with?"

The captain pulled out his pen knife and folded out a corkscrew. "Will this work?"

Jake carefully turned the corkscrew into the stopper as the divers joined them. He pulled out the cork and there was a loud pop and the savory smell of rum. Everyone smiled as the captain brought out plastic cups. Jake took the first sip, wondering if it would kill him.

"*Whoa*! That is smooth. Yes, it is definitely okay to drink. Yo ho and a bottle of rum!"

They all slowly sipped the rum, enjoying the smooth tangy flavor. "It warms your innards, mates."

"So, how many bottles are down there?" the captain asked.

"Not sure, at least two or three crates," John replied. "We'll have to carefully remove the bottles one at time, load them into baskets, and hoist them to the surface. And there are crates of this honey, too."

Mary Lou removed the heavy wax seal on one of the jars. A thick and dark goo was inside. "We better check this out more carefully. I don't want anyone to get food poisoning. Smells okay, but it is pretty thick and a dark color," Mary Lou said as she collected the jars and the bottles and took them into the cabin.

"That's it for today, Captain. We'll get more equipment from the warehouse and return tomorrow." Smiles swelled and remained on everyone's faces.

Chapter 6

Bryn Mawr

"So, how did it go?"

Gloria came into the living room with her travel bag, looking glum.

"Oh, not so good? Come sit down here. Do you want some tea, or a stiff scotch?"

Gloria laughed. "Let's start with tea and go from there." She sat on the couch, staring out the window at the Pennsylvania countryside as the sun was setting on Sunday night. Using the microwave to heat the water, Sophia was back in a minute with a large cup of lemon-scented tea and some of Gloria's favorite chocolate chip cookies.

"You sure know how to treat a girl. How was Petr?"

"Every Sunday is hard. We have such a great time together and I miss him so much. But we knew how our marriage would go for at least a while, so I keep up my spirits waiting for the next weekend."

"Any discussion of moving Petr's lab down here, or you moving to the Boston Veritas office?"

"We talk about a lot of future plans, but for now we are okay with this. We have some time before we need to make those decisions. I may move to Boston but not for a while. Now, how about you? How was the Big Apple?"

Gloria smiled and groaned. "It was the best of times, and the worst of times. Somebody said that once and they were right. On the romance side, it was fantastic. He met me with a bouquet of red roses and then dinner and then a movie on the couch and then the talk and then the sex. Other than the talk, it was heavenly. A lot of good sex. He cooked breakfast—he is a great cook. We toured the Museum of Natural History and he knew so much about so many of the exhibits. He's really smart. Funny, too. I love him, Sophia, and I miss him so much it hurts.

"But the talk did not go well. I told him right up front that I knew what he really does. He told me that it was like an addiction, not easy to break. He also talked about some German who is blackmailing him. So, that said, redemption did not seem to be in the cards. We agreed to set the issue aside and enjoy the weekend and we did. My heart is aching to see him again; my brain is telling me firmly that it is not going to work out."

Sophia gave her a hug. "You did it right, girl. He knows the score and you do, too. Enjoy it as long as you can and then walk away when it doesn't work anymore."

"The thing is I understand that addiction feeling. It took solitary confinement with the FBI, a crazy president threatening to kill me, a daring escape from the White House, and Jake Beaucour to the rescue to cure me. I thank God every day that my new life uses my old skills to do good things. When I get that tingling feeling to outsmart someone, I am still feeding the addiction by helping others for a good cause."

"Hey, I used to beat up people and ruin their lives for that *la puttana* in Italy, and I really enjoyed the physical part of it, punching out somebody. That's why I joined the Italian army special forces unit, to be the best fighter in the world. But that general aimed me in the wrong direction and working for that bitch just became my life. The Egyptian pharaoh's arrow in my chest and her betrayal with Interpol smacked me upside the head, and I saw the light. I thank Jake Beaucour every day for the chance to do good with my skills. I know what you mean."

Gloria took a deep breath and sighed. "Moving right along, any word on Rabia?"

"Nothing. All the intelligence reports say the Bomani are overrunning the country. Women are being tortured and imprisoned. Many of the elderly are being executed. The children have been collected and sent to indoctrination camps. These dudes are nasty and I can't understand why the United States abandoned these people."

"We can't get into the politics. That's somebody else's problem. But don't you wonder where Rabia is? I can't imagine a strong woman would just sit still and get caught up in all of this. Why doesn't she contact us?"

"I've been sending her two or three messages each day, so the opportunity is there. Right now, I guess she doesn't want anyone to know where she is."

*　　*　　*　　*　　*

And, Sophia was right. Rabia did not want anyone to know where she was. She had moved into the mountains around Bulcan, organizing and fortifying her three clandestine bases, each supporting four hundred armed and highly trained women, ready for a fight. Her days were filled with meetings and planning missions to challenge the Bomani to drive them from Mandragostan. While she planned, her troops trained.

Over the past three years, Rabia had purchased more than ten thousand weapons and hundreds of thousands of rounds of ammunition. Her strategy team had outlined several scenarios for destroying the Bomani if they returned. The first line of defense at the border had not worked but the strategists had analyzed why and knew better ways to approach the next phase.

"We have planned several attacks similar to the way the Bomani attacked us. We will bomb their warehouses, find small groups and kill them, and interfere with their supply lines. We will also work to disrupt their power grid."

"I appreciate your planning and we may have to resort to that kind of guerrilla warfare. But, I am thinking much bigger. If we could find a way to get most of them in one place, we could destroy their army. Have one big fight rather than many skirmishes."

"I see your point. We could just level the city, bomb it into oblivion. That would kill most of them."

"Yes, but that is the saying 'burn down the barn to get rid of the rats'. If we did that we would kill thousands of our own and destroy what we have built. We must think of a place and reason for the Bomani to gather together. When do they ever come together?"

"That is a part of their strategy, to always stay in small groups, and that is why the United States could not defeat them. They are like rats with many nests."

"Then let us think what would bring these rats together in one place. What would be the bait?"

*   *   *   *   *

"Mr. President, we are watching the situation in Mandragostan."

"Why is that little country so important?" the president replied. "Why were we even there? It was a stupid waste of time and resources."

"And the loss of twenty-five brave men and women in our armed forces, sir."

"Yeah, that too. I think we will just let that situation work itself out. We gave them so much. If they don't want to be free, fight for their rights, protect themselves, then that's too bad. They get what they work for."

"Sir, we can have ten thousand troops on the ground within twenty-four hours. We can force the Bomani out of Mandragostan again and restart the new life that we helped to create in that country."

"Nah, I don't see wasting any more money and time on that place. Let it go." There was a pause. "And we don't want to lose any more of our people there, either."

"But sir, the harshness of this group, the treatment of women and children, murdering the elderly, the violation of human rights. How can we sit by and allow this to happen? We should stop this senseless brutality."

"Look, we aren't getting much of anything out of helping this little country. The American people want us out of there. Let it go."

"But sir."

"What part of NO do you not understand? Let's move on to something more important than this little African country. How is our 'Save the Beaches' campaign going?"

Chapter 7

Norfolk

As the sun rose over Norfolk, the friends made their way to the boat. Today would be the day they had been waiting for, pulling the gold chests from the sunken wreck. John had loaded several baskets tethered with a special rope designed for heavy loads and lined with a fine net to catch anything that broke loose. He also brought smaller containers in case the chests of gold broke open. The crates were in such bad shape, he expected the chests to give way as well.

The captain greeted them with a broad smile and guided the boat to the GPS location. John explained the operation to Molly and Jake, and then he and his two assistants dove into the water as Mary Lou, Molly, and Jake lowered the baskets. The divers guided the baskets to the wreck and began loading the baskets with the rum and honey, hoping to clear enough space in the hold to remove the chests. As each basket was ready, they signaled the crew; the crane hoisted the basket, the people on deck emptied the baskets into new crates on deck, and then the baskets descended to begin the process again.

With the necessary diving breaks, it took the entire morning to clear a pathway to the chests, but as John swam through the hull, he couldn't locate the crates. He shone his search light around the area and saw piles of broken wood. The chests were gone. "What the hell?" he shouted into his mask.

"John, are you okay?" Mary Lou asked.

"Someone has taken the chests. There's a pile of rotten wood from the crates and the spot where the three chests rested is empty. Gone."

Mary Lou pulled Jake aside. "You need to be ready, now. The only person who knew where we were and what we were getting is our captain. He came back and took the chests or he told someone else to do it. There's no other way this could have happened. Watch out—for this much gold, people have been killed."

Jake called Molly into the cabin. "You two wait in here."

Jake stepped out of the door and the captain swung an oar at his head. Bad move. Jake deflected the oar and broke the captain's leg with one kick. The captain collapsed onto the deck screaming in pain, "Oh God, you broke my leg! Oh God!"

"You tried to crack my head open." Jake set his foot on the captain's chest, pressing just enough to cause pain. "You will tell me right now where the crates are."

The captain continued to scream. "Get off of me, you're breaking my ribs! I can't breathe!"

"It will be more than broken bones if you don't tell me now." Jake pressed a little harder. The captain writhed around, trying to break free, then reckoned Jake was too strong and concluded he could not escape.

"He said he would kill my family, my wife and my children. He offered me five thousand dollars. I had no choice. Please!"

Jake let some of the pressure off. "Who is 'he'? Give me his name."

"He didn't have a name, just a text message. I sent him the GPS coordinates. I didn't know what you found but he said whatever it was, he wanted it. Please, please, you must believe me."

"You tried to kill me. Why shouldn't I throw you overboard right now and let the sharks finish you off?"

"My phone. Get my phone from the counter! I'll show you."

"Molly. Mary Lou." The two came out of the cabin. "Grab his phone."

Mary Lou handed the phone to Jake and he put it in the captain's face. The captain touched the screen with his thumb and the phone opened.

"Look at the text messages." Jake lifted his foot off the captain who gasped for air, groaning and tentatively caressing his broken leg.

Jake scrolled through the messages and found what he was looking for. He texted the message and address to Veritas and typed: "Need immediate identification. Need Sophia and Gloria ASAP in Norfolk at the warehouse. Returning to port. You know what to do."

Jake tied a rope around the captain's fat belly and then tied him to the crane. He waited for the divers to surface and climb aboard. As Mary Lou explained what had happened, Jake gunned the engines and headed for port. At maximum speed they were at the dock in forty minutes. The police and an ambulance were ready for the captain. Jake threatened the captain to say nothing about the text messages or the bribe. "Tell the police you had an accident and broke your leg and we helped you back to port. Unless you want to go to prison for grand larceny." Clenching his teeth, the captain nodded. When asked, he recounted the tale of his unfortunate accident for the record.

John's two assistants helped move the baskets of rum and honey into the warehouse and then left. John said he would be in touch. The couples huddled around the computer monitor and watched the video again. There was no question that the three crates had been smashed and chests were gone.

"These had to be professional divers," John explained. "Stealing these in the dark with the currents, the unstable wreckage, and the weight of the fifty-pound chests would require sophisticated tools and at least three people, someone on the boat and two in the water. Is there any way to find out what boats might have left this harbor in the past twenty-four hours?"

Molly said yes and began tapping the keyboard. "There's a website that logs all boats entering and leaving the harbor. If they came from here there should be a record." A list of twenty-three boats appeared on the screen. Eliminating the boats too small to handle the salvage weight, two Navy destroyers, and one cruise ship, nine possibilities remained. Five had gone out but only four had returned.

Gloria and Sophia arrived as Molly finished printing the list including the ships' docks. As a group they reviewed everything they knew with the two agents. "We know the thieves got the GPS location from the captain," Sophia said, "but how did they know what you were looking for. Who knew?"

"I only told Mary Lou, and Jake didn't tell anyone," Molly said.

"I never told anyone what we were looking for," John added. "I explained to the two divers that we were exploring a sunken ship but when we found the rum and the honey, I intentionally did not mention the chests."

"John and I have discussed this mission at length but I haven't mentioned any of this to anyone else," Mary Lou chimed in.

"Well," Gloria said with some hesitancy, "think about the wedding. This was a topic of discussion at the party in Cesky. Who might have heard that conversation?"

"Molly and I were talking about it, then you and Noah joined us. I didn't see anyone else. I guess Noah heard about it but he seemed like such a nice guy, I can't imagine he would be behind this."

"I only learned about this expedition yesterday and I didn't share it with anyone," Sophia said. She looked at Gloria.

"Jake, can we talk over here."

"Sure. Why don't you all start calling those docks and find out more about the boats that went out, especially the one that didn't return."

Gloria and Jake stepped outside. "What's up?"

"I need to tell you about Noah." Jake squinted with curiosity. "I realized at the wedding that Noah was a professional fence and cat burglar I worked with ten years ago in my former life. Interpol calls him 'Sir Hood'. I have been struggling with my personal feelings toward him, and my professional duty to my job and to you. I have been trying to figure out if he is still in the game, and when we were in New York, he said he was.

"This situation reminded me that his eyes lit up for just a second at the wedding when Molly and Mary Lou were talking about the boxes of gold. I'm afraid he may be the thief."

"Oh, Gloria. Do you really think it could be him?"

"Unfortunately, yes. He listened very closely to Mary Lou and Molly and then tried to pump me for information at the wedding dinner. I avoided sharing anything because I saw that look, and he backed off.

"When we were in New York, he tried again. After I told him I knew who he was, he didn't mention the search again but he was in the room when Sophia called and he might have heard her say we were headed to Norfolk. He may have been following Mary Lou since the wedding. I don't know, though I have that gut feeling that he is behind this."

"Okay. If you have any contact with him, pretend you don't know anything. Play along with him. Can you call him? We could trace his phone signal if you could keep him on the phone long enough."

"I can try but he's very savvy and will probably know what's up. I am so sorry, Jake."

"Gloria, these things happen and you couldn't have known. At least we have a possible lead. I hope you are wrong about this theft, and I hope Noah will agree to go straight. We can talk about that later. For now, we need to concentrate on finding the chests."

"Can I ask, is this just about the gold, or is there some greater value to these chests, something historical?"

"We didn't get to look inside the chests, so we don't know for certain. Indications in the journal suggest the gold was in the form of coins, so they would probably be ten-dollar Gold Eagle coins. The Gold Eagles are worth around a thousand dollars apiece. If we price the chests at gold prices, they are worth approximately four million dollars. If each chest contains a thousand Gold Eagle coins, then we are looking at around three million in collector value. Either way it's a lot of money."

"Yeah, a lot of money. That's what Noah said before I told him I was on to him."

"Let's see what everyone has found and then track Noah's phone."

They joined the rest of the group at the table. Mary Lou and John contacted the four ships that had left port and then returned. Three of them were clearly pleasure cruises for tourists. The fourth was a deep-sea fishing expedition, but that could be a cover.

Molly had delved into the fifth ship, the one that had not returned. It was a charter and had the capacity for salvage operations with a crane hoist and a large deck. It was rented to a Herr Donovan, paid in cash, and its destination was Cape Charles on the Virginia Eastern Shore.

"That's it," Gloria announced. "Donovan is the guy in Europe who is blackmailing Noah. We need to get to Cape Charles before they take off with everything."

Jake called a friend from his Navy SEAL days who arrived ten minutes later in a helicopter that landed on the water off the dock. All six scrambled into the chopper and were off to Port Charles.

"Hello, Commander. Good to see you. We are on a routine training flight and I'm glad you're along for the ride. We should be to Port Charles in about thirty minutes."

Jake acknowledged the welcome and thanked the pilot for responding so quickly. He handed binoculars to Molly and Mary Lou who were sitting at the windows on each side. "Look for any ships with a crane and possibly cargo on the deck."

As the chopper approached Port Charles, Mary Lou spotted the boat. "That one, Jake. The crane is right and there are three boxes on the deck near the back." Jake directed the pilot to the dock area where he let them out and then left. Mary Lou stood on the dock watching for the boat while the others backed into the shadows. No need to have a large greeting party.

As the boat pulled up to the dock, Mary Lou casually walked away. She didn't want anyone to recognize her and she wanted to be out of the way if there was trouble. Sophia, Jake, and Gloria appeared with guns drawn. Once the boat was tied to the dock, the three stepped out from behind a large crate and aimed their guns at the crew.

"Good morning," Jake yelled. "I believe you have something that belongs to me."

One crew member reached for something on the deck and Gloria shot his arm. He fell to the deck screaming in pain. "Anyone else want to try something stupid?"

Sophia boarded the boat first, making each of the three crew members lie down, tying their hands behind their backs with zip-ties. Then she zip-tied their feet together. She also tied a rag around the crew member's wound. "That should do for a while."

Jake and Gloria boarded the boat and opened one of the boxes. They found the chest inside. The other two boxes also contained the chests. They were still wet.

Jake went over to one of the crew and put his foot on the guy's leg. "I don't ask questions twice, so I better get an answer the first time. Or . . ." His boot pressed the leg into the deck and the crew member knew it would break.

"Okay, all right, what do you want to know?" he cried.

"Who hired you to do this?"

"Only name I got was Noah, no last name."

"Where were you taking these boxes?"

"There's a golf cart over there with keys. We were supposed to load the three boxes into the cart and drive to Warehouse Fourteen, down that way." The crew member nodded his head down the docks. "Then we were supposed to disappear."

"How did you get paid?"

"Noah handed us cash in Norfolk before we started, and said he would give us more cash when we delivered. There's supposed to be an envelope on the cart."

"So," Jake continued, "you three are going to stay here on the boat. We have a sharpshooter who is watching you. If you step off the boat, you're going down. Any questions?"

"Yeah," the second crew member asked. "Who the hell are you and what's in these boxes that you're willing to steal them from us?"

"I'm the person you stole those boxes from, and it's none of your damn business what's in them or who I am. Let's go."

Gloria and Sophia lifted each box onto the dock. The crew did not move but watched as the boxes were loaded onto the golf cart. Sophia threw the envelope of cash into the boat and waved goodbye. They drove down the dock toward Warehouse Fourteen.

"Do you really think he has a sharpshooter watching us?"

"I'm not dumb enough to find out. Why don't you get off the boat and we'll see what happens to you?" No one moved.

Chapter 8

Port Charles, Eastern Shore

"Donovan, that was too easy," Noah said into his cell. "I followed the archaeologist right to the dock, paid the captain for the GPS coordinates, sent three guys to get the boxes, and they are on their way here now. I should have four million in gold coins in no time. You bring me the videotape and I'll give you the gold and we're even. I'm done with you. You have your big payout."

"We made a deal, Chambers," the thick German accent replied. "I will see you in the Baltimore Hyatt parking garage, level two, at eight tonight. We will complete the transaction."

"Good. The golf cart is arriving here now." Noah hung up and proceeded to the doorway. First, he noticed that there was no driver. Then he noticed there were no boxes. He retreated in the shadows of the warehouse and felt the gun barrel on his neck.

"I think you made a big mistake, Noah Chambers," Jake said in a gravelly voice. "You don't take something that belongs to other people. Turn around slowly."

Noah knew Jake's reputation and knew Jake could kill him in an instant. There was no way he could escape. He turned very slowly, bowing his head, respecting the gun pointed in his face. "I'm not sure what you are talking about, sir."

"I was really hopeful for you and Gloria. You seemed so perfectly matched. She won't be happy when I tell her about this." Hidden behind a large shipping crate in the shadows of the warehouse, Gloria and Sophia listened.

"Okay, now wait a minute. I have to get the gold to Donovan in Baltimore tonight. He's going to trade an incriminating security tape for the gold. Once I have that tape, I can quit this business and start living an honest life. And as for Gloria, I really do love her. I . . . it's . . . complicated."

Jake growled. "You expect me to believe that nonsense? Interpol has been looking for you for over ten years. That's a lot of crimes, a lot of money, a lot of ingrained habits. You're not going to give it up and you can't be that stupid to think that Donovan is going to give you some tape. He probably has ten more copies and will call you next month with your next job. You can't give it up and he won't let you."

"I have a plan."

"Oh, I'm sure you do. Turn around, hands behind your back." Jake used zip-ties, pushing Noah out into the sunlight. John was waiting for him and he shoved Noah into the backseat of the cart. "So, you're the scumbag who stole my chests. Let's get out of here, Jake."

*   *   *   *   *

The last thing Noah remembered was a prick on his shoulder. *They must have drugged me.* He sat up, hands still tied behind his back, surveying the room, assessing his situation. It looked like a classic Hollywood scene, a darkened room with one lightbulb hanging from the ceiling, one chair facing him. Jake Beaucour walked out of the shadows and sat in the chair.

"Now, you're going to tell me about Donovan, what he looks like, how much security he keeps at his side. Where's the meeting and what's supposed to go down. Spill it all now."

"Look, if Donovan lives beyond tonight, I'm a dead man. He doesn't forgive or forget. I can't let you ambush him and put him in jail; he has to die. My plan is to meet him in the parking garage of the Hyatt Hotel at the Inner Harbor. I'll show him the three chests of gold, he'll hand me a videotape, and I'll shoot him before he realizes what is going on. His two henchmen will be looking out over the walls of the garage for the police. By the time they realize he is dead, I will kill them as well. Then I get in my car and drive away with the chests and the video. Simple plan and it is done."

"You've got it all figured out."

"Yeah, I do. I've been doing this for a long time. Just let me go and give me the chests and this will be over."

"That simple, just give the con man the gold and everything will be fine. Of course, Donovan is so stupid that he would never think you would double-cross him, so he won't have an extra person nearby to take you out when you make your move. And if you succeed in your move, I'm sure you will bring the chests right back to me. Right?"

"What do you need that gold for? You've got plenty of money. I promise I will return it but if I don't you will survive. And if Donovan double-crosses me then what do you care. I'm out of your hair."

"I can see Gloria means a lot to you."

"She does mean a lot to me. I have never felt this way about any woman but our lives are traveling in two different directions. I know she is on the right path and she is dedicated to it. That won't change and I applaud her for that. She is lucky to have you on her side. I would never do anything to change her.

"I have to do the changing and I just don't see me doing that. I can say I'll quit but I know in my head that I won't give up that easy money. People are just too gullible. And I'm not going to live a constant lie just to be with Gloria. That's not fair to her.

Some day she will probably be hunting me for stealing something from one of your clients. I hope that never happens."

Jake stared at Noah and then disappeared into the darkness.

"Hey! You can't just walk away. Come back! I need to get to Baltimore!" There was no answer. Noah struggled to free himself but it was no use. He waited for an eternity.

*　　*　　*　　*　　*

The six met in a nearby office in the warehouse. They had all heard Jake's interview with Noah. "Thoughts, folks?"

"We don't give him the gold, that's for sure," Mary Lou said. Gloria agreed.

"Can we take care of Donovan?" Molly asked. "Surely he is a recognized criminal around the world."

Sophia turned her laptop to the group. "He is very good at covering his tracks. Arrested seven times and freed every time without trial or penalty. He has significant blackmail leverage on several high officials in Interpol and local police departments as well. Deep pockets also help to pay officials to look the other way. Two police chiefs have tried to apprehend him and both are dead. 'Accidents' as the newspapers report."

"Jake, he's a bad guy. Why not let Noah take him out?" John asked. "Our interest in this whole mess is the shipwreck and the chests of gold. We really don't care how the rest plays out."

Jake turned to Gloria. "I feel awful putting you in this dilemma, Gloria. If you don't want to be part of this, please feel free to leave."

"There is no dilemma, Jake. I told him and I will tell you and Molly that Veritas comes first and everything else has to bend or break. I asked him to give it up and he said he would think about it. Clearly, things didn't go my way in that daydream.

"I would suggest that you give him the chests filled with rocks or something else to make them heavy. Let him think he has the gold. Let him go to the garage and if he returns the chests to you, maybe that's a redeeming step forward."

"And what if he's killed?"

"He seems to be resolved to whatever his end may be." Then she whispered in Jake's ear, "I think that Sophia and I should probably go spend the night in the Hyatt." Jake knew the look in her eye, the cunning one that said she was ready for action.

Jake turned to the group. "Okay then. Mary Lou, you and John make the switch on the chests of gold. Something heavy. Then let's load them into his rental car. Sophia, you should take Gloria away from all this, maybe spend the night in a local hotel or something." He winked at them. "Just be careful about getting involved in anything local. You know the drill. Molly, I need you to talk to Noah with me. Everybody okay?"

They all agreed. Mary Lou and John got busy with the chests, Sophia took Gloria by the hand and left while Jake and Molly headed across the warehouse to Noah. Jake told Molly to lay it on thick about Gloria and going straight. She would be the good cop, the friend, the confidante. Jake would play hard, threatening Noah's life if he cheated on Jake. Jake walked into the light.

"Oh, thank God you are here. I have got to go now. I don't even know where I am. I've got to get to Baltimore."

"Here's the deal, Noah. The chests are in your car. You're already in Baltimore. We brought you here while you were sleeping, so you've got plenty of time. Your gun is in your glove compartment, loaded and ready. Whatever happens is on you. I just want the gold back. Don't make me come after you because I won't send Gloria. It's your choice if you go down the straight road or the crooked one. Just stay away from Veritas clients."

Jake stepped out of the light and then Molly stepped in. "Hello, Noah."

Chapter 9

Baltimore

Sophia checked them into a room at the Inner Harbor Hyatt and the two agents discussed the plan on the way to their room. Noah had shared the time and the parking level for the swap. They planned to be nearby, and an hour before the meeting time they entered the garage.

Donovan told Noah to go to the ramp between levels two and three. He would be waiting in a black SUV with an orange cone behind it. They would exchange the chests and the video and then leave.

"Just in case he brings some extra guests, I'll go near the top of the ramp. You cover the bottom of the ramp. Then we should have it all in crossfire." Both agents had suppressors on their guns so as not to draw attention to their positions if they opened fire. They tested their coms by calling into Jake, who was outside the garage watching for the arrivals. "Be careful. This German is supposed to be ruthless and unforgiving. Things could get ugly. No action yet out here. I'll let you know when the party gets started."

At 4:45 a convoy of SUVs approached the garage entrance. "You've got company, three incoming." The first vehicle climbed the ramp to the third level and parked at the top. The second pulled into an open space about halfway up the ramp; the driver placed an orange cone behind the car. The third parked at the bottom of the ramp.

"Three clowns down here," Sophia reported.

"Two up here."

Just before five, Noah drove into the garage and climbed to the ramp. He saw the orange cone and parked his rental behind the SUV. A big muscular guy got out of the SUV and aimed a gun at Noah. Noah climbed out of the car with his hands in the air and the bodyguard searched him. "He's clean."

The driver got out and opened the back door for Donovan who was dressed in a suit, perfectly manicured, a real noble gentleman. He straightened his tie, snapped his sleeves, and stepped to Noah's car. "Let's get this done," he said in a thick Slavic accent.

Noah opened the trunk and pointed to the three chests. The driver looked them over while the bodyguard continued to hold a gun on Noah. The two at the top of the ramp got out of their car and stood at attention, the three at the bottom did the same.

Noah looked up and down the ramp. "Hey, I don't want any trouble here," Noah said. "Just give me the tape and you can have the chests and we're done."

"We're done when I say we are done," Donovan growled in response. "Move the chests into the SUV." The driver and the bodyguard picked up one chest. It was heavy and a real struggle for the driver who dropped the box into the rear of the SUV with a thud. "Gerard, you must do more exercises and eat healthier foods. Look at Erik. He could probably lift the boxes by himself." Donovan smirked and chuckled at his own wittiness.

The men lifted the second box and loaded it into the SUV. As they reached into the trunk to pull out the third chest, Noah slammed the trunk lid down on the two; the crunch and screams indicated at least one of them was hurt pretty badly. Noah turned on Donovan and pulled out a knife from his sleeve. As he ran at Donovan, the bodyguard recovered and pulled his gun. Noah dove under the SUV as the bodyguard shot Donovan in the chest.

The two at the top of the ramp started running down to the SUV. Gloria stood up and shot both of them in the head; they dropped instantly. Sophia did the same at the bottom and the five thugs were finished. The driver had been killed by the trunk lid and lay on the ground behind the car, blood pooling around his head. Donovan was dead, a bullet piercing his heart. The bodyguard was enraged by his stupid mistake and his own injuries hurt like hell. He started shooting wildly, trying to kill Noah under the SUV. Not even thinking in his rage, he shot through the gas tank and the SUV exploded sending pieces flying in all directions. Gloria and Sophia instinctively dove for cover.

As soon as the initial blast was over, Sophia came running to Gloria and pulled her into the exit stairway. They made their way to the entrance of the hotel, smoothing their clothes and looking calm and respectable. They walked to the elevator and returned to their room while the sirens outside became many and intense. Fire engines sped into the garage as the police cordoned off the area. There was a second explosion—presumably a second car had caught fire.

Jake was on his way back to Bryn Mawr when he called his agents. "Everything okay?"

"We're back in the room," Sophia replied. "We shot five, looks like Noah killed one, and the other two were killed in the explosion. When they sort it all out, they will know that there were guns involved. We made sure all the security cameras in the garage were disabled, so no trace of us. We don't know if Noah got out or not. He was rolling under the cars when the SUV exploded."

"How did that happen?"

Sophia described the whole incident explaining how the bodyguard had shot the gas tank causing the explosion.

"Wow! Lucky the entire hotel didn't burn to the ground. Let me know if you hear from Noah. We'll see you back in the office tomorrow."

*　*　*　*　*

When the agents arrived at Veritas the next morning, Jen Crockett called them into her office. "Glad you all are safe. No word on Noah?"

"Nothing," Gloria replied. "If he survived, we will probably never hear from him. If he didn't, it was his death wish."

"We'll see." Jen paused and then handed a folder to Gloria. "I need to share some strange news with you about Mandragostan."

"Have you heard from Rabia?"

"Not exactly but something is going on. The Bomani are holding a large rally tomorrow at noon. Sandorian, the new Khadir, has called all the Bomani to a gathering in the city's stadium to celebrate their victory. He has invited international news coverage, so we'll be watching at six in the morning. Peculiar because the Bomani never have large gatherings. El Cadiz would never allow it . . . but of course he is dead. Sources say Sandorian is so confident in their victory that he feels he can do this celebration once to show the world he has no fear of outside intervention. He's even using the stadium that the United States built for the citizens of Mandragostan to show the world the U.S. is no longer in charge."

"Interesting, but how does this concern Veritas?" Sophia asked.

"Two ways. First, Rabia Begum is a Veritas client. I need you to prepare an extraction plan and form a team if she requests help. We still have not heard anything from her but with this rally she may finally see that she needs to get out."

"Even though we haven't heard from her in the past two weeks, you think she is still in Mandragostan?"

"She's a client," Jen asserted, "and Veritas must be prepared to help a client if she requests help from anywhere in the world. I can't imagine what she is doing, though I sure hope she is out of that country or in a very good hiding place. Why would she want to stay there with the Bomani in charge?"

"Probably loyalty to her citizens," Gloria replied. "In our discussions with her, she was very loyal and often talked about fighting the Bomani if they invaded. Who knows? The Bomani seem to have taken firm control of Mandragostan. I don't think women have a chance there anymore."

"In your extraction plan, make it very clear to our team that we will not be taking any prisoners. If the Bomani interfere with the extraction, they are to be eliminated.

"Now, the second thing. I got a call from the CIA. The President's National Security Team wants to know if there is any possibility of enlisting people in Mandragostan for counter-terrorism measures. They know we have a close relationship with Rabia and they want to start up an underground network to harass the new leaders."

"Nobody's talking about just taking out this bunch of self-centered heathens?" Sophia asked.

"I asked if the U.S. would consider invading again. The answer was a blunt 'No, the president does not want to engage.' I think that about sums up the current administration's position on Mandragostan."

"Humph, so much for women's rights."

"Not our call, ladies. Veritas is trying to avoid any involvement with the Washington establishment. I think I will tell them it will take more aggressive responses than underground harassment, and Veritas is not interested in setting up a terrorist network in Mandragostan, even if it is on our side. I just wanted you to know in case someone from Washington approaches you."

"Thanks for the heads up. We're going to head home for a few hours," Sophia said. "Baltimore was tough in more ways than one and we need some rest." She glanced at Gloria and Jen understood.

*   *   *   *   *

"Your royal highness, my Khadijah, sire. How may I assist you?" The head of security bowed in reverence to the Bomani leader.

"I have decided that our men deserve a celebration of our victory," Sandorian announced. "We will use the stadium that the Americans built for these Mandragostan pigs and we shall gather all the Bomani together. There will be music and dancing, food and drink, and women as their rewards. Lots of women, virgins."

"Sire, it is my duty as head of your security to question your decision for the good of you and all your men. Is it wise to bring all our troops together in one place?"

"There is no one left to challenge us. The Mandragostan army fell apart, ran away, or we executed them. No one else can stand up to us."

"You are right, sire. But what if the United States decides to attack us? Are we not easy targets, gathered all together in one large place? Again, it is my duty to ask these questions."

"And you fulfill your duty to me and the Bomani wisely. I take no offense from your questions. I have a personal promise from people within the American government that they will not be attacking us or interfering with our rule. Trust me on this one. I know."

"Then if you have these guarantees, sire, you should proceed with a most magnificent celebration. I will arrange the details."

The announcement was sent out to all the people of Mandragostan to stay inside their homes on the celebration day. Only the Bomani were permitted to walk the streets and congregate in the city's massive stadium. The Khadir commanded all virgins come to the square outside the stadium for further instructions, requiring them to wear the light blue robe of virginity. The celebration would commence at noon the following day. News media across the globe were notified as well and invited to broadcast the Bomani's video feed.

Chapter 10

Mandragostan

The Veritas intelligence team met at five-thirty the next morning to watch the rally unfold in Mandragostan. Twenty thousand men loyal to the Khadir marched into the city's stadium, built by the United States for the people of Mandragostan. Television news crews were banned from the stadium and were forced to use the official feed of the Bomani. Bands were playing music and tables of food and drink surrounded the playing field. Guards at the four entrances only permitted the Bomani to enter. The terrorist television coverage gloated on their victory and the defeat of the United States.

As Sandorian stepped forward on a raised balcony, the crowd erupted in cheers. He stood at the podium with the emblem of the Bomani, a fist holding a saber ready to strike, projected behind him. He began his speech and translators relayed his words to the world.

"We have conquered Mandragostan." The crowded cheered again until he raised his hands. "We are mighty. We are strong. We will dominate the world." More cheers. "We are bringing back traditional values to the world. Women will learn their place at our feet. The elderly must work hard to pay for their care. Children will be trained as loyal soldiers. We will cleanse the world of these ignorant old people, these rebellious women, and these ill-mannered children." He pounded his fist on the podium as he said each group.

The camera scanned the crowd on the stadium floor and then moved up to the top as many women covered from head to toe in light blue robes surrounded the rim of the stadium. "Ah, you can see our slaves above you in their blue robes of virginity," Sandorian continued, laughing. "They are here to meet your needs. These are the first prizes of your hard work and dedication to our cause." The Bomani down in the stadium went wild, cheering and stomping and then singing a familiar song about a woman's place in their lives. Many men used obscene hand gestures at the women to insult them, and some stripped naked to show off their manhood, waving to the women to come and enjoy their loins. As the chorus began for a second time, the worldwide television coverage suddenly went dark but the audio continued to broadcast. The world sat stunned by what they were hearing.

*　　*　　*　　*　　*

Rabia's strategic team had planned every step of their attack with great detail and caution. They were ready when the Khadir announced his celebration. Teams of twenty women moved into Bulcan in staggered groups from four different directions. They met in a warehouse that Rabia had stocked with weapons and supplies months before the Bomani had invaded.

Each of the thousand women in Rabia's army wore her uniform with bullet-proof vests beneath and each was armed with a high-powered rifle, a handgun, and a knife. They knew what to do with each weapon. They donned the light blue robes of the virgin required by the Bomani.

"How convenient that they chose long robes that cover everything," Rabia commented to her deputy, Dalia Nsia. "Each team leader knows her part. Move out."

Groups of twenty robed women moved through the neighborhoods to the square outside of the stadium, obeying the Khadir's orders to appear. So many men were entering the city for the celebration that the small groups blended into the crowds. The Bomani were determined to reach the stadium to hear the Khadir speak, and they moved quickly through the streets ignoring the wretched people.

Three hundred blue-robed women congregated in the nearby plaza awaiting a signal from one of the Bomani commanders to encircle the stadium ramparts. They were reminded they were sacrifices and their duty to submit accordingly. Demurely, the women bowed their heads in acquiescence. "We know our duties to the Khadir; we are here to serve." The commander sneered and led the accursed to the top of the stadium.

Rabia looked down upon her enemies, thousands of men appallingly shouting, strutting, celebrating. She watched as Sandorian stepped to the podium and she listened intently to his speech. Her strategists were certain the Bomani would sing their filthy song about a woman's place in the world, the second chorus a signal to her troops. The Bomani danced about making crude gestures at the women surrounding the top of the stadium. Many were exposing themselves to show what they would do to the women. Rabia chuckled to herself: *your puny parts will be of little use in a few moments*.

The Bomani began to sing the song, verse one describing the lowly lives of women serving men by cooking and sewing and cleaning. The disgusting chorus announcing the dominance of man and the slavery of women was next. Rabia's troops were angered by these insults, their adrenaline rising with each word.

The second verse was even worse, describing what men would do to women, their dominance over women's bodies, their animalistic rights. And then the second chorus began.

Rabia watched as several of her women cut the wires to the cameras and then slit the throats of the cameramen. The crowd continued singing not perceiving what was happening above them. As the chorus ended and they started the third verse, explosions sealed the four main exits. All the guards were killed by the bombs. The Bomani turned in panic to see all three hundred virgins dropping their blue robes, standing in full military gear raising their rifles to their shoulders.

The massacre began.

Two hundred sharpshooters systematically slaughtered the thousands below them. Another fifty women shot grenades into the crowd killing hundreds at a time, a bloodbath as thousands were annihilated within a few short minutes. And then, cannisters of liquid shot through the air into the crowd, igniting when they hit the ground. Every man in the stadium was incinerated, not one surviving the inferno. Five minutes from start to finish—almost twenty thousand men destroyed.

Realizing he was under attack, the Khadir and his security guard retreated into the bowels of the stadium. Rabia's second in command was waiting for them with fifty support personnel. The guard hustled Sandorian into a saferoom, a concrete bunker beneath the stadium designed to protect visiting entertainers, sports teams, and dignitaries from terrorist attacks and bombing raids. The room was fortified and the guards blocked the entryway, unaware that Rabia's forces had already prepared the room for them. As the guards sealed the doors to prevent poisonous gas from entering, there was a loud ticking sound. Everyone froze as Sandorian yelled, "What is that sound?" He received his answer as a bomb exploded followed by the same engulfing flames from the stadium. Rabia's forces waited at the doorway for anyone who might try to escape. No one did.

The remaining six hundred women in Rabia's army were already spreading out across Mandragostan. Their assignment: to find any Bomani who did not go to the stadium and eliminate them.

As they moved through each village, the people would point to the houses where the Bomani were hiding. Within minutes, Rabia's troops terminated them. The people cheered the soldiers as they marched on to the next village.

Some of the Bomani in the countryside heard of the stadium attack and realized they were in danger. They thought the United States was returning, so they ran for their hideouts in the mountains. Rabia's strategists had expected this. In a very clever ploy, the fleeing men were funneled into one checkpoint where ten men, loyal to Rabia, pretended to be Bomani members. They pinned a medallion on each of the fleeing men's shirts. "This will protect you. If any of those women find you, they will see the medallion and know you are loyal to their new leader. This will give you safe passage to the mountains. The Bomani shall rise again." The fleeing men eagerly accepted the medallions as shields and raced into the mountains to their hideouts.

They did not know that each medallion contained a tracking chip. Rabia's strategic team watched on a computerized map of the region where every terrorist went. In two days they knew where the few remaining Bomani were hiding out in six camps deep in the mountains. Groups of fifty women were dispatched to each of the camps. They surrounded the hidden settlements and pummeled the remaining men in the same way they had annihilated them in the stadium. Each camp was eliminated.

Within hours of the stadium battle, Rabia spoke to her country and to the world in a televised newscast. "My name is Rabia Begum. Today, my army of professionally trained women has defeated the Bomani. As a loyal Mandragonian, I pledge to you that the Bomani will no longer harass our nation, torture our women and children, or disrespect our elderly. They have been eliminated.

"I also pledge to you that as we restore order to our country over the next several weeks, we will be organizing elections. I encourage any citizen who would like a role in the new government to speak with our election committee to be put on the ballot.

"I am also speaking to the world community. Mandragostan does not want any interference by foreign powers, no foreign aid, no troops, no weapons. What we want is recognition as an independent country and inclusion in the world community as equals. During the past ten years, we have established a modern country and a successful economy. It was temporarily derailed by the Bomani. That was corrected today. We expect to return to normal business over the next several weeks. Foreign interference will not be tolerated.

"In closing, my fellow Mandragonians, may God bless our nation and guide us in the future growth of our country and our children."

*　　*　　*　　*　　*

The world sat in horror listening to the attack. They had no idea what was happening. The screams, the explosions, the sounds of gunfire were clearly some type of attack. After five minutes of darkness, an image suddenly appeared on the screens around the world. It was a woman, dressed military-style, with armor and weapons at her side.

"I am Rabia Begum, a loyal citizen of Mandragostan. The people have taken back our country from the invaders. The Bomani no longer exist. Look upon their demise and know of our determination to remain free."

The picture changed to a panorama of the stadium, the world witnessing the total annihilation of the Bomani. While some reacted with horror, most of the citizens of the world cheered on the women. Social media lit up with slogans and support; GoFundMe pages were instantly at work, raising funds to support the new army. The world had no idea of the power she was wielding against the Bomani, but when the floor of the stadium ignited, everyone knew an evil force had been dealt a deadly blow.

Veritas staff were stunned by what they were seeing. "Oh my God," Sophia began, "she used everything we taught her, Gloria. Each tactical move, every weapon. I can't believe she has done this."

"It doesn't surprise me, Sophia. She was determined right from our first meeting to learn everything about tactical attacks. We thought we were training her security team but it looks like we were training her commanders to train these women. I wonder how many of them there are?"

Jake motioned to Gloria and Sophia to follow him. Jen, Rich, and Molly were already waiting in the conference room, watching the events unfold. As the door shut, they stood and applauded. Gloria and Sophia looked confused.

"Have a seat," Rich said, motioning to the chairs around the table.

"Did you know this was going to happen?"

"The answer to that question is no and it will always be no even when Congress asks it," was Jake's response.

Jen took over. "We knew Rabia Begum was not interested in fleeing her country. We knew she purchased over ten thousand guns and other weapons with plenty of ammunition and a thousand military uniforms with bulletproof vests, but she was smart and did it over a three-year period in small quantities. Our intelligence community did not pay any attention. She was preparing years before the U.S. withdrawal and the Bomani invasion."

Rich continued. "We thought she was forming an underground movement to harass the Bomani, in the same way the Bomani had harassed Mandragostan. None of us saw this coming. The clue that something bigger might be happening was the purchase of the thousand blue robes. That occurred at one time two weeks ago and we were pretty certain Rabia was not going to submit to the Bomani and their warped sense of male domination."

"But," Jake said, "you did exactly as you were assigned to do by Veritas, you trained her security team. None of us are responsible for what happened today. And don't be surprised if there are questions hurled in our direction by Congressional wimps who didn't have the guts to do this themselves."

*　　*　　*　　*　　*

The Secret Service agents moved into the Oval Office quickly. "Sir, there is a potential threat and we must move you to the bunker immediately."

"Ah, com'on. I just got my grilled-cheese sandwich for lunch. Why do we have to move down there?"

As the two agents gently but firmly lifted the president from his chair, he stood up and began to walk. "Okay, okay. I get it. You have a job to do. I'm moving." He turned to one of his aides. "Make sure my lunch gets down there pronto."

As the president sat down at the conference table in the bunker below the White House, he asked, "So, what's the big emergency?"

"Sir, the actions in Mandragostan are very disturbing. Our threat level has escalated to red due to a massacre led by Rabia Begum."

"Wait a minute. A massacre? You're telling me I had to move down here because some woman tried to kill off her enemies?"

The Secretary of State, the Joint Chiefs, the Secretary of Defense, and the rest of the National Security Council entered the bunker taking their places around the table. The president looked around the room. "Quite a party we've got here. What's the big deal?"

"The big deal, as you put it, sir, is that an army of one thousand women just annihilated an army of twenty thousand terrorists in less than an hour."

"What? What the hell happened there? I thought the Bomani were going to restore law and order after their invasion. Somebody just murdered all the authority in the country? Now it's going to be a wild west show. How the hell did this happen?" The president was red in the face, pounding his fist on the table, glaring at his advisers.

"Mr. President, we told you about this mass celebration meeting in the stadium and we advised you to attack and destroy the Bomani in one bold move. You refused and we let it drop at your direction."

"*Goddamnit*, Ernie. I don't want the United States running around the world trying to remake every little screwed up nation. We had no business being there in the first place and returning was not an option. This was their problem to solve. We better not have helped with this, I commanded no involvement. Who is this Begum woman?"

The Secretary of State shifted in his seat. "Sir, Rabia Begum is an extremely wealthy, highly successful Mandragonian. We couldn't ask for a better ally and we should recognize her as the interim leader and offer her immediate support. She has already pledged to have free and open elections once the country has calmed down."

"To hell with that. So, some rich broad took over the country. How long will that last? We will have to send in at least ten thousand troops to quell the uprising. Those men will be back."

"No, sir, we are not sending in any troops," the Secretary of Defense replied. "She has just annihilated twenty thousand terrorists; the Bomani will not be returning. She specifically and forcefully said she does not want any help from anyone. This is a good thing, sir, and you need to listen to our advice."

The president sat staring at a news monitor on the bunker wall, his elbows on the table, his hands in front of him, fingertips to fingertips as if in contemplation. "All right, if that's what you say, then do it. Let's move on. Where is my sandwich?"

*　*　*　*　*

"Madame Speaker, we must hold hearings and investigate this Mandragostan issue. We were preparing a House declaration of support for Sandorian the Khadir and now this happens. There is no way some woman, even if she is wealthy, could have done this alone. Someone helped her and guided her army. They probably even supplied the weapons. What foul group is behind her? This is an international travesty, that a woman could overthrow the leader of a country."

The Speaker of the House paused, looking over her reading glasses at the three representatives sitting across from her. "Are you kidding? First of all, Sandorian was a serious enemy of the United States, an international terrorist. We would never recognize him as a legitimate leader and he would not receive any support from us. Whoever took him out deserves a Congressional Medal.

"Secondly, gentlemen, throughout history there have been many successful women warriors leading armies and defeating empires. Go the library and read about Joan of Arc, the Valkyries in Scandinavia, Boudica of the Celtics, the pirate Grace O'Malley, and Zenobia of Syria to name just a few. Rabia Begum clearly had the upper hand on these men and beat the crap out of them. More power to her."

"But, Madam Speaker, the United States cannot be outfoxed this way. We must investigate and find out how this happened. Our party depends on it."

"What some of you depend on are the donations to your campaigns by friends of that Khadir thug. If you pursue these hearings, you may find yourselves deep in the mud. You're the Chairman of the House Committee on Foreign Affairs, so you can go ahead and start your hearings. But I'm warning you, I will not be supporting any media attack on Rabia Begum, and the media may dig just deep enough to expose your connections to the Bomani. Watch out—I will not have your back."

The Chairman of the Foreign Relations Committee bristled at her mention of his contributor connections to the Bomani. The representatives left in a huff as the Speaker called in one of her best investigators, Michael Drude.

"I want you to keep a close eye on Representative Gorman. He's treading on very thin ice and I don't want the rest of us associated with his half-assed ideas. Find out who helped Begum defeat the Bomani."

"Yes, ma'am. Right away."

Chapter 11

Bryn Mawr

Sophia knocked on Gloria's bedroom door. "Are you still up?"

Gloria opened the door and invited her in. "Still searching for Noah. I call his phone every day. No answer, just the answering machine. I've asked Veritas to track down his phone, but so far it has been turned off. I've been surfing the Internet, even digging into his websites in the dark web, and there is no response. If he's alive, he's gone dark."

"Well, we know he's alive from the security camera footage at the garage. We clearly see him walking away from the garage right after the explosion. He is somewhere but he probably doesn't want anyone finding him anytime soon."

"I can't decide if I want to find him anytime soon. Do I hug him or arrest the bastard?"

*   *   *   *   *

The Baltimore incident had not gone according to Noah's plan but he was rid of Donovan and his henchmen, and . . . he was still alive. He wasn't sure if there were others in Donovan's operation who would want to kill him, so he laid low for a few months and watched carefully for bounties on his head and investigators asking lots of questions. Noah had only two contacts–the man who maintained his estate and the woman who managed his finances. Neither knew of Noah's real career; they were handed money to do their jobs and didn't ask where the money came from. Noah had to contact them.

When all hell broke loose in the garage, Noah had instinctively rolled under the SUV. Knowing he couldn't stay there he quickly rolled under two more cars before crouching and then running away from the scene. When he reached the exit door to the stairwell, the cars exploded. He slid through the doorway slamming the steel door behind him. He heard metal pounding into the door.

Down the stairway and onto the street, he walked slowly and calmly away from the situation. Two blocks from the hotel, he crossed Light Street to the Inner Harbor promenade and leisurely walked to his hotel. Once in his room, he took a couple of deep breaths, got in the shower, changed clothes, put on a baseball cap and sunglasses, and took his duffle bag full of passports, cash, and disguises.

Noah checked out of the Four Seasons Hotel and hailed a cab, traveling to the Penn Railway Station north of the Inner Harbor. The original plan was a flight out of BWI to Europe but he was worried that booking a last-minute flight and the scan of his face for international travel might expose him. The train was much safer to make his getaway. He found an overnight express to Sanford, Florida. That seemed a good place to get lost in the tourist crowds.

He was able to rest on the trip south and by morning he was feeling refreshed and ready for the next part of his journey. He had shut down his phone in Baltimore to avoid any electronic tracking but decided to make a quick contact to his two important people. He sent a text to both, *check your email for further instructions*, and shut off the phone again. At the Sanford train station, he found a cab.

"Where to, sir?"

"Port Canaveral."

"That's a hundred-dollar fare, sir."

"That's fine. Let's go." Noah threw his duffle bag into the seat and climbed in. The trip to the port took an hour and when he arrived, he asked the cabby to drop him at Grills, one of the dockside restaurants. He went to the Tiki bar outside and found a stool.

"What'll you have, mate?" the bartender asked in a strong Australian accent.

"I'll have a Bloody Mary, and some information."

The bartender delivered the drink and leaned on the bar. "This ain't no tourist information booth," he smiled. Noah placed a fifty-dollar bill on the counter. "What might you need to know, mate?"

"I need a quick trip to the Bahamas on a small boat, not a cruise ship. Got any ideas?"

The bartender picked up the fifty, looked around the bar for anyone listening, and said, "Not too far to swim, mate, but give this guy a call. He runs 'charters' for folks who are willing to pay five hundred."

"Thanks. Can I use your phone?" The bartender passed his phone to Noah. "And here is another fifty for the use of the phone. Thanks."

Noah called Jamal de Mariner. "Hello?" the voice answered with a thick Caribbean accent.

"I am in need of a charter trip to Freeport, now. Are you available?"

"That would be five hundred, plus a hundred for the rush. You at Grills?"

"Yes."

"I'll be at the boat ramp in twenty minutes. You?"

"Baseball cap and sunglasses. Tom is the name."

"Of course it is." The phone clicked dead.

"Thank you for your help. And here is another fifty for forgetting you ever saw me."

"Saw who?" The bartender smiled again as he pocketed the third bill.

*   *   *   *   *

Gloria and Sophia arrived in the Veritas cyber center at eight in the morning. Pam greeted them with a big smile.

"Good morning, ladies. I have some good news for you. Come over here." Pam led them to a large monitor near her desk. "Your suspect was very smart and turned off his phone in Baltimore. However, his last call was a text to two people when he arrived in Sanford."

"Sanford? Like Florida? Why the hell would he be in Sanford?" Sophia could tell Gloria was on edge since she usually didn't curse this much.

Pam continued. "We have traced those two names and they are his financial adviser in Paris and the man who maintains his estate in southern Spain. Simple message, *check your email for further instructions.* We will monitor their email accounts and keep checking for his phone but chances are he won't use it again. At least you know he made it that far."

"Thank you, Pam. Sorry to be so grumpy but this guy really has me in a twist."

"I understand. Been there myself. My suggestion would be to review any security footage from the train station. You might get lucky."

Sophia and Gloria stepped into their office and started cyber sleuthing. Gloria got into the security cameras at the Sanford station within minutes. "Will you look at that?"

Sophia leaned over. "What?"

Gloria pointed at the video on the screen. "There's our boy getting into a cab. He hasn't even tried to disguise himself. So, does he want us to find him, or is he just being a cocky jerk thinking he's scot-free?"

"Look, you've got the cab company and the cab number. Should we call them?"

"Takes too much time to convince them to help. Probably have some privacy policy and they can 'only give out information to police'. I'll get in there and find out where he went."

Ten minutes later, keys clacking away, Gloria said, "Bingo. Cab 762 took its passenger to Grills in Port Canaveral. Noah is on vacation."

"No. Think about it. If he can get to the Bahamas, he can go anywhere in the world without being identified. That would be my guess, Freeport or Nassau."

"Let's check out Grills." More keyboard work and the security cameras at Grills came online. "He's not in the restaurant. I'll try the bar." More clicks. "Ah, there he is, schmoozing the bartender. Several dollar bills going down on the counter . . . a business card. Let's see." Gloria clicked several more keys as she zoomed in on the video image. "Too fuzzy, can't make out the phone number."

Sophia studied the picture. "That's a J-a-m-a-l. That's all I can make out. Give me the phone number for the restaurant." She dialed the number and asked for the bartender.

"Yeah, hello?" the cocky Australian voice answered.

Sophia spoke in perfect Spanish. "I am looking for Jamal. Do you know where he is?"

"Who wants to know?"

"I am his little girlfriend and I am really worked up, ready for some action. I need to see him right away."

"Well, missy, you'll have to cross your legs for a while. He's just pulling away from the dock with a customer."

"Another trip to Freeport?"

"Yep. Gotta go, *senorita*." The phone went dead.

Chapter 12

Freeport, Bahamas

"So, you've tracked him to Freeport?" Rich asked on the phone link to Veritas.

"We know he's on a boat right now racing to Freeport. If the boat goes thirty miles per hour, it's about one hundred seventy miles to Freeport, so it will take about seven hours. He left at one this afternoon, so he should be in Freeport by eight."

"And once you locate him, what is the plan?" Jen asked.

"That's what I wanted to talk to you about. He obviously has a long history of crimes but is he currently under investigation for the Baltimore mess or could he be charged with anything from that?"

"Okay, let's take this one step at a time," Rich said. "There are many choices here. Veritas really doesn't have any interest in Noah Chambers. The gold from the shipwreck chests is secure in a Veritas vault, and as far as we know, Noah has not compromised any Veritas client. We are not going to report him to Interpol and we don't care about him."

"You have to make some choices and we will back you up," Jen said. "If you are not interested in Noah, then we let him go, he disappears and lives his life as he wants. Who knows, he might show up here sometime in the future.

"If you are interested in him, you can wait for him to come to you, or you can pursue him. The question would be, when you find him, what will you do?"

"I won't speak for Gloria," Sophia said. "But it seems to me that we should at least let him know somehow that Veritas is not chasing him, that the Baltimore incident has not been traced to him. Can we offer him redemption through Veritas?"

Rich and Jen shared a glance. "Rachel Dixon's indiscretions died with her in a motorboat in Greece," Rich said. "Your indiscretions were forgiven because you testified and put your Italian fashion designer away for life. I don't see the same path for Noah. What can he offer in exchange for no jail time?"

"We could consider it," Jen continued, "but that would be down the road a piece with legal advice and a lot of work on Noah's part. We can't commit to helping with that now. Of course, if Noah were to do that on his own, that would be his business. Technically, I guess he blew up in that bomb in the garage. We wouldn't want to know his new identity. If you want to use the small jet to get to Freeport, it is at your disposal."

Gloria put her head in her hands, elbows on the table. She wept quietly as Sophia rubbed her shoulders. "I owe you all so much and I swear I will never go back to my Rachel days. I don't want to jeopardize who I am now. My problem is, I love him. I have never felt this way about anyone. When we are together, it is so magnetic, so close, so much within me. I don't know what to do. I really don't."

"This has to be your decision," Jen said softly. "I can tell you that finding the one person who makes your life whole is so important." She squeezed Rich's hand. "You should go to him and at least tell him he is free from Veritas's eye. Tell him how you feel and what your limits are with his schemes. I can only tell you again that Veritas will not pursue him as long as he is not messing with our clients."

Sophia held Gloria's hand. "It's time for us to go."

Gloria stood and said, "Thank you for the jet." Fire and Ice were out the door, on their way to the Bahamas, and with a little luck, they would land before Noah reached the dock.

*   *   *   *   *

"We've got some updates to share with you." Jake and Molly were sitting at the conference room table waiting for their weekly briefing.

"First, we have heard from Rabia Begum," Jen shared. "She is requesting help from Sophia and Gloria. We think this is a straight business deal, providing expert security help to a client. They will travel to Mandragostan next week."

"Good," Molly answered. "Leave it to a brave woman to handle a situation like this. We should provide whatever she requests. Do we have to tell the government about this?"

"We checked it out with legal," Rich continued. "We can do business with a private citizen without contacting the State Department. Our government has not recognized her as the leader of Mandragostan yet. If she becomes an elected official in the country, then we have to report our work with a foreign country."

"We can hope she will be elected as the leader but at least we can help until that happens."

"Second, the police in Baltimore have determined the explosion in the garage was a drug deal gone bad. It's amazing to me how they can create a whole scenario based on one piece of evidence. You were right, Jake. The police forensics lab did find the trace amounts of heroin that our evidence team planted in the wooden chests. The explosion destroyed the chests, but there were some fragments with heroin residue. The resulting story is two guys in a car pulled up to buy the heroin from the dealer who was killed alongside the SUV. The two guys from above and the three from below were on opposing teams and during the gun battle one of them shot the gas tank and it exploded. No evidence of Noah."

"That's lucky for him," Jake observed.

"Third, Noah Chambers. Gloria and Sophia have tracked him down to Freeport. They are in the small jet right now hoping to intercept him there."

"Is Veritas pursuing him?"

"No," Jen continued. "There is no evidence connecting him to any crimes against our clients. This is a personal thing for Gloria."

"Not an easy thing," Molly replied. "I have never seen Gloria lose control over anything but this guy has really knocked her for a loop. She really loves him."

"I don't have any problem with her personal love life," Jake commented, "but I am concerned that Noah is taking her for a ride, using her. She was the connection on the chests of gold. Have we found out anything about him?"

Rich and Jen described the information that Veritas had collected—financials, homes around the world, two business associates, no family or personal friends, a real loner, five known aliases, his dark website where he advertises his services, and Interpol's thin file with little information. "It's hard to know if he is serious about Gloria or taking advantage. I guess we'll know more when they get back."

"No apprehension of suspect?"

"Nope."

*   *   *   *   *

Noah's boat trip was approaching the Freeport Harbor as the Veritas jet landed at the nearby airfield. The agents knew this was a gamble because there were hundreds of islands in the Bahamas and plenty of docks in Freeport. The bartender had said Freeport, so that was why they were here. They arrived at the main docks at seven, hopefully an hour before Noah would show up.

"Are we almost there?" Noah asked Jamal.

"We will be there at eight, as I have told you several times. When we reach the wharf, I will tie the boat to the dock and talk to the customs people who are personal friends. You must leave the boat while my friends are looking the other way. If you miss the opportunity, you will have to deal with the authorities. I will be on my boat, out of the harbor."

Noah knew he meant business: get off the boat and good luck.

*   *   *   *   *

Sophia and Gloria surveyed the dock area, perhaps two hundred yards long with many opportunities to land. "How are we going to cover all of this?" Sophia asked.

"It's pretty quiet with just a few boats coming and going. I have an idea." Gloria took her laptop and climbed on top of a large cargo container. "You walk down there about a hundred yards and then act like you are getting out of a boat and crossing the open area."

Gloria aimed the camera on the laptop at Sophia. She activated a facial recognition app on the laptop and waited. At first, Sophia was a blurry blob on the screen. As Gloria made adjustments in the camera program, her image became quite clear and then the software pinged with Sophia's file. "Got it!" Gloria yelled. Sophia hiked back to the container.

*　　*　　*　　*　　*

Noah could see the dock coming into view. Everything looked pretty quiet. *Good, not too many people to deal with.* Jamal docked the boat smoothly, jumping out to tie the front and then the back. "Good luck, *amigo*." He walked across the dock parking lot to the two guards in the dimly lit guardhouse.

"Is that him, walking across the parking lot?" Sophia whispered.

"No, look at that guy's beer gut. Not even close. But what about this shadow?" Noah slowly climbed over the side of the boat and slowly walked up the ramp. Gloria turned the laptop to focus on the dark image. The ping was instantaneous. "Got him. Let's go."

The two slid down the container and split up, Sophia walking along the edge of the dock near the boat, Gloria circling inland through the containers.

Noah turned the corner around one of the containers and came face-to-face with Gloria. He jumped back in fear and then recognized her.

"What the hell?!"

"That's no way to greet an old friend."

"I don't want to hurt you, Gloria, but I'm not going back, I'm not going to prison. Let me go or I'll have to use this." Noah pulled a knife out of his belt. "I mean it."

"First of all, you know and I know that your knife would be useless in a fight with me. Secondly, no one is here to take you anywhere."

Sophia stood quietly behind Noah. He didn't know she was there. He held the knife up and then sighed and lowered it into its sheath.

"Veritas has no beef with you as long as you stay away from our clients. Baltimore police have ruled that the mess in the garage was a drug bust gone wrong. They don't know you were even there."

"Why would they think it was drugs? Wouldn't the gold tell them otherwise?"

"Noah, you don't think we would really let you take four million in gold and give it to that German jerk, do you? The chests were full of metal slugs and dusted with heroin. The explosion melted most of the plugs and left enough heroin residue for the police lab to decide the chests were full of heroin."

"I never had the gold?"

"Sorry, we couldn't trust you with that, and I guess we were right."

"I had a plan, Gloria. I was able to disarm the two henchmen who were with him and then I killed Donovan. I was going to roll under the cars and then come up and take back the car with the chests. Then there were five other guys with guns blazing and then the explosion. I decided it was time to get out of there."

"He doesn't even know we were there, Sophia," Gloria said as she looked beyond Noah. He turned and saw Sophia.

"I'm going to go over there and wait. You two have some things to talk about. Noah, one wrong move and you will not see the sun rise tomorrow." Sophia disappeared into the shadows, actually moving closer to the two.

"Veritas has checked with Interpol. They are still hot on the trail of Sir Hood but no mention of Noah Chambers. You are safe and can go home. I love you Noah but I don't like you as a thief. You will make your choices. I hope I will be one of them, though it must be up to you. If you decide on a straight life, making money hand over foot with our investments, I'll be waiting in Bryn Mawr. But if you must continue your life of crime, then stay away from any of our clients and stay away from me. That's it."

Gloria stepped back into the shadows ready to leave.

"Wait a minute. Wait a minute. I get my say in this," Noah spoke intensely. "I have never loved any woman before you. I cannot explain the attachment I feel to you. I want to live the rest of my life with you and I will try to find my way back to you but I cannot promise you I can do it. Gloria, if we don't talk before this date next year, I want us to meet here, in the shadows of these containers, to talk again. I believe you Americans call it 'Same Time Next Year'. At least we can have that one day each year when we can put our real lives aside for a day and a night."

"Interesting idea, Noah. I hope to see you sooner, but I'll definitely see you here, the same time next year." Gloria looked unsure, sad, and then faded into the shadows. Noah stood in the dark contemplating what had just happened.

Fire and Ice were gone.

Chapter 13

Bryn Mawr

It was six days after the stadium battle in Mandragostan and a lot had gone down in that time, though Gloria and Sophia were finally getting back to their normal schedule. Sophia's phone was ringing in the kitchen and she ran across the room to answer it.

"Hello, Sophia? It is Rabia Begum."

"Oh, Rabia, it is so good to hear your voice. Let me get Gloria." Sophia yelled up the stairs and Gloria came bounding down two steps at a time. "I'm putting you on speaker."

"Hello, Rabia! Way to go, girl!" was Gloria's greeting.

She could hear Rabia chuckling. "So, my friends, how is this playing out in the United States? I have received congratulations and thanks from many countries but your president has not called. The Secretary of State called and offered assistance. I thanked him and said I would contact him when I needed it."

"I know the Italians will support you one hundred percent," Sophia shared. "We hate these terrorist groups. I've been very pleased with the response by the American people. No one has protested against your actions and many groups are praising you for your firm approach to terrorists. Your GoFundMe pages seem to be raising a lot of money to support your new government. Some politicians are suggesting the U.S. government should learn from your actions and take steps to annihilate these terrorist groups around the globe. You are something of a hero here."

"Yeah," Gloria continued. "The video coverage was a bit alarming, seeing a massacre live can be disturbing. But I think it sent a strong message that you weren't messing around or compromising. Freedom was non-negotiable. This was final. Good for you."

"At the moment," Rabia said, "we are in good shape. As one does with an infestation of rats, we are exterminating the last of them in the hills. Your tracker-in-a- lapel-pin was a superb way to track every one of them. Now we are re-establishing our government functions and working on getting the economy up and running. My strategic council is doing a fantastic job; nevertheless, I need some eyes from outside to advise me on some of our next steps. The election is especially important.

"I want to let the people choose their leaders, but I want to be sure that some conservative fanatic is not elected. We cannot afford election trickery and we will not go backwards. I need your ideas on how to do the election correctly while protecting what we have saved. Can you come here in the next few days?"

"I'm sure we can. We just have to check with Rich Crockett since he is our boss. I will ask the obvious question, Rabia. Are you well-protected, safe from harm?"

"I am as safe as one can be in an unsettled situation. My personal guard surrounds me at all times and our location is secure. We have eliminated most any group attack, though we must be vigilant for a lone assassin. Thank you for asking, that is the kind of reflection I need. I hope to see you both soon."

*   *   *   *   *

"Okay," Jen reported, "our lawyers have negotiated with Rabia's people and the contract is set. Everything is legal and above board. You will need to go through Egypt since our State

Department has not lifted the 'no go' provisions on Mandragostan yet."

"Is there something going on in Washington that we need to know about?" Sophia asked. "I would think your government would be dancing in the streets and praising Rabia. Why not?"

"We're investigating that very quietly," Rich said. "So far, it appears there is a small group in Congress that have received large sums of money in the past from the Bomani. They were preparing to recognize the Bomani as the official government of Mandragostan but Rabia's move put an end to that."

"Why would anyone in our government support the Bomani?" Gloria asked.

"Same old thing, follow the money. And I think some of these Congressmen think women have too much power. They don't like the Speaker and want to replace her. She's very powerful right now, and the Mandragostan situation has strengthened her position. If word leaked to the press about these Congressmen, their careers would be over."

"And the president?"

"That's a real quandary," Jen chimed in. "You would think he would jump at the chance to show his support for women around the world. We can't seem to figure that one out yet."

"Our focus is on fair and secure elections," Gloria said. "We'll work with Pristine International on the voting process. They have implemented our security protocols perfectly and I think elections run through their process are clean and proper. As to any candidates, as we get names, we'll forward them to Veritas for a full examination."

Fire and Ice were on their way to help a friend set up a new nation.

Chapter 14

White House

"Where is my peanut butter sandwich?"

"Sir, the kitchen is preparing it and it will be here soon."

"How long does it take to spread some peanut butter on some bread? And be sure it's grape jelly. I don't want any of those yucky preserves."

"Yes, sir." The president's aide rolled his eyes as he stepped out of the Oval Office to check on the food and the Secretaries of State and Defense stepped in.

"Good morning, Mr. President."

"Yeah, yeah, let's get on with it. What's wrong in the world today? Anymore massacres by wild women?"

"Sir, we are pleased to report that the world is calm today. So far, no terrorist incidents, no changes in governments, no weapons deals, or other problems. We are here to discuss Mandragostan."

"Oh brother. Really?"

The secretaries looked at each other with quizzical looks. *What is going on with this man? He's president of the United States and acts like he doesn't care. Very strange.* The look suggested a meeting later to discuss the behavior they were observing.

The butler knocked and stepped into the Oval Office with a tray. "Sir, your sandwich and some tea."

"Thanks, Fred. Set it down here." The secretaries knew the butler's name was Thomas and he was politely ignoring the president's mistake.

"Ah, peanut butter." The president smacked his lips as he bit into the sandwich.

Another look of surprise between the secretaries. "Sir, the State Department strategic council has determined Mandragostan presents the United States with a unique location in Africa to monitor many insurgent groups in the area. We believe we should make an offer to the new leaders for an alliance and our support. Then we can establish a base of operations."

"Not this again. Come on, man, give it up. We have already put several billion dollars and ten years' worth of military support into that place. All of that and some woman takes over? Shows what that bunch is made of."

"Sir, from a military standpoint, they executed a brilliant plan. From an economic point of view, they are bringing that country back online in record time. The world is watching them with amazement, and some people are saying that maybe women should be in charge of the world."

"Hah, you don't think they already are? Do you do anything in your household without your wife's approval? Sometimes I think the First Lady is running the country and I'm just following orders." The president snickered.

Another look of surprise and concern was exchanged. "Sir, we all joke about our wives but they are very important partners in what we do. We have many women leaders in our country today—governors, senators, representatives, cabinet members. I think we are far beyond the old male idea that women should stay in the kitchen. Your party has supported women's rights for years and worked to promote their political careers."

"Okay, okay, I'm sure you are right," the president said as he rolled his eyes. "What can you tell me about this new government, these women in puny Mandragostan?"

"This is what our intelligence has been able to collect so far." The secretary handed a red folder to the president, who thumbed through the pages. His mood seemed to change.

"Weapons were all purchased legally from many sources over the past three years. Smart. We weren't paying attention to that.

"A thousand women trained as sharpshooters, hand-to-hand combat with knives, bomb experts, right under our noses. And then what they did to those men? They were clever, and we weren't watching their actions.

"Begum financed and led the whole thing. We know where she got her money but no idea on how they were trained?"

"Reports suggest three secret bases in the mountains and a core training group who taught all the others these skills, sir."

"Okay, but who trained that core leadership group? We need to know if it was a friend or a foe. Do we need to worry that she will lead her country in the wrong direction? Is she just going to be the next dictator?"

The secretaries looked at each other and nodded their approval. *Now he sounds like a president, right on target with the right questions. What changed?*

"The CIA is trying to find out about that, sir. So far, no one has been identified."

"I think that would be a topic of discussion with the Begum group," the president responded. "And reassurances that women's rights, that all people's rights will be protected."

"Yes, sir," the Secretary of State replied. "I will dispatch the former ambassador back to Mandragostan for discussions."

"All right, gentlemen. Keep me apprised of what you find out. Perhaps I need to call her in the next few days and welcome her to the world community of leaders."

*　　*　　*　　*　　*

"I am telling you, Sarah, it was a bizarre meeting. One minute he was complaining about a peanut butter sandwich and hurling insults around the Oval Office about women. Then there was a sudden change to a serious, on-the-ball, in-charge president. I'm not sure what that was all about."

Sarah Mixson, head of the CIA, was meeting with the Defense Secretary and the director of the FBI over lunch in the Langley rooftop dining room. The view of the Potomac below and Washington in the distance was stunning in the afternoon sunlight.

"Philip, we have had some recent concerns about the president's mental health. We have discreetly asked his doctors about it, and they have firmly denied any physical or mental problems. The doctors went so far as to say we should ask the First Lady if we wanted to know anything. Needless to say, the First Lady is not returning my calls."

"We'll keep an eye on it and report more concerns to you. We may have to approach the vice president about this."

"We need to take this slow and deliberate. Any challenge to the president's fitness to serve will be met with a hailstorm of criticism. There will need to be a serious and very public stumble to convince the cabinet. And unfortunately, it is very clear that the First Lady will fight us every step of the way. Be very careful."

The FBI Director agreed and encouraged the Defense Secretary to talk privately with cabinet members that he trusted. Treasury would have to know and the Secret Service would need to weigh in as well. This was a very difficult position for the nation to be in. Was the president mentally fit to fulfill his duties?

"So, I need information on how this Mandragostan army was trained."

CIA turned to the FBI. "Your turn."

Don Bangs explained that the FBI was not involved in international incidents but they were trying to find out if any United States citizens were involved in the Mandragostan situation. "The last time Rabia Begum met with anyone from the United States was almost four years ago. Two agents from Veritas worked with her, training her security detail and preparing defenses against possible terrorist attacks."

"As a rich, powerful, and independent woman," Sarah continued, "Begum was a target of the Bomani and also the conservative religious group, the Meglans. The Bomani sent a hit squad to attack her residence. Her security team killed them all and piled the bodies in the street for everyone to see. The Meglans sent another group to kill her in her limousine. Her convoy slaughtered all twenty assailants instantly, leaving another pile of bodies in the street. The message got out very quickly that she was not messing around. In a third attempt, both groups worked together to break into her residence and take her hostage. Once again, a pile of bodies in the street.

"When the U.S. pulled out and the Bomani invaded, she disappeared. No one could locate her for almost four weeks. The Bomani overran the capital and in his typical cocky fashion, Sandorian declared a national day of celebration in the stadium, and we know how all that turned out. Begum had prepared for that day for three years."

"And executed her plans brilliantly."

"Her army was trained by her own people, homegrown," Defense noted. "But the initial training came from Veritas, a loyal partner of the United States in keeping the world safe."

"I see no need to share that information with anyone," the FBI said. "There is no need to get the media and Congress all hyped up over this. Begum needs to be the hero, the highly intelligent person who put this together. Where she learned how to do it is not important. We need to assure the president and the American people that she is not connected to any of our enemies. That's all."

"To be honest, she could have learned most of this stuff over the Internet. But Veritas probably sent their best to train her people."

"Such an efficient and effective army, and clearly, she has an amazing group of strategists to plan that kind of ambush. The Bomani played right into her hands. Keep me posted on the president's mental state."

*　　*　　*　　*　　*

"Madame Speaker, as required by House rules, I am informing the Representatives that the Committee on Foreign Affairs will be holding hearings on the Mandragostan situation. We must determine how a group of uneducated women were able to amass an army of one thousand highly trained individuals to slaughter twenty thousand men. The United States cannot be seen as a nation builder, training military groups to overrun the established leadership in charge of a country."

The raucous objections in the House were intense, many shouting insults at Representative Gorman. One even shouted 'traitor'. Before the Speaker could respond, the Minority Leader stood to be recognized.

"Madame Speaker, this is the most absurd proposal I have seen in years. We cannot in good faith waste millions of taxpayer dollars on this farcical witch hunt. Obviously, the Congressman from Ohio does not realize that the Bomani were mortal enemies of the United States, pledging to overrun our own nation. We lost over fourteen hundred brave soldiers to their terrorist attacks during the ten years we helped Mandragostan establish its place in the modern world. No one in their right mind can consider the Bomani the legitimate government of Mandragostan.

"The Congressman has no regard for the safety and the rights of the women and children and the elderly that the Bomani sought to subjugate and torture. These proposed hearings are a travesty and I move for a vote by the House right now to stop these hearings."

The Speaker pounded her gavel and stated the motion to the full House, staring directly at the Chair of the Foreign Affairs Committee. Several representatives seconded the motion. The Speaker invited discussion and only one other Representative stood to speak.

"There is no need for any further discussion, Madame Speaker. This is a ridiculous request by the Foreign Affairs Committee. Let the public record show very clearly if any representative would support such an un-American activity." The House erupted in applause and the Speaker gaveled the session back to attention.

"I will invite any discussion one more time before we vote. Anyone?" She paused for thirty seconds and no one stood. The Foreign Affairs Chair was sure his party would rally behind him and he stood proudly as the Representatives voted and the tally was announced.

"The house has voted," the Speaker announced. "Yeas, opposing the hearings, 402. Nays, supporting the hearings, 12. Abstentions, 21. The Foreign Affairs Committee is denied any hearings on the Mandragonian matter."

Chapter 15

Bryn Mawr

"Wow," Rich exclaimed, "I don't think the House has ever voted like that. Over four hundred of them denying the hearings. Good news for Veritas. Our lawyers can stand down."

"It is good news. Any word from Gloria and Sophia?" Molly asked.

"All we know right now is they got to Mandragostan. I've asked for a daily briefing, which would be dinnertime for them and breakfast for us. I hope to hear something tomorrow morning and I'll keep you posted."

"Been a busy two weeks here," Jake observed. "All the Mandragostan stuff, finding the gold in the shipwreck, the Baltimore explosion, tracking down Noah Chambers, the House vote, and now more Mandragostan drama."

"We have made arrangements to convert the gold coins to cash," Jen reported. "The purchaser agreed to pay the going rate for gold, and we agreed that he could sell the gold or the coins as he saw fit. I think he is going to sell the coins to collectors in small quantities. In the end he should come out ahead. Four million, two hundred seventy thousand dollars was anonymously donated to the Shriner's Children's Hospital Network. Mission accomplished."

"Our financial department did the investigation into François' fortune in Québec," Rich continued. "After quite a bit of digging, they finally found his actual will with the official embossed stamp of the city of Québec. Here's a translation." Rich handed folders to Molly and Jake.

"As you will read, his estate was divided into four parts. First, the trust of five hundred thousand dollars, to preserve the warehouse, which has grown through the years to over seven million dollars, as well as preserving the building. Second, his taxes to the city including a charitable donation on his part to thank Québec for his life and his success. Another five hundred thousand dollars. Third, he donated five hundred thousand to a children's hospital in Québec. Unfortunately, the hospital was not cooperative in sharing what happened to the money but you can be assured that he gave it with the best interests of the children. The last five hundred thousand was designated for gifts, distributed by the bank. These included cash awards to the owner of the inn where the Beaucours spent their first days in Québec; to the families of his two loyal employees who worked for François for more than forty years; to the police department that had let his sons go free; a sum was sent to France to his family in Beaucourt; and finally, two small accounts of ten thousand dollars each were set up in François Jr. and Jacque's names. Both of those accounts are waiting for members of the two families to claim them. Estimated value after one hundred thirty years is over five million dollars."

"Please have the legal department close that account and give the money to the same children's hospital fund. Also, have them notify William Johnson about his account. He can decide what he wants to do with it."

"That ties up another loose end."

"Which brings us to the gold bar," Molly pointed out. "We know how seven of the bars ended up but François Jr. had one more bar that we cannot trace. Did you all find anything?"

"Pam worked on it for some time," Jen explained. "She searched through every one of François' bank accounts, loans, donations, even the contents of his safe deposit box when he died. Nothing."

"I wonder if it is still at the farm, hidden somewhere?" Molly pondered.

"Sounds like a great mystery novel or treasure hunt."

"Sounds like a vacation in Illinois and some snooping around. Only this time we let the Morfords know we are coming so they don't try to shoot us."

*   *   *   *   *

Molly and Jake made it a habit to call their two sons on Sunday afternoon every week. Jacob, the eldest, was a successful corporate lawyer living in Boston with his wife and two boys. Ethan was an accomplished artist, painting landscapes of the National Parks and other famous monuments, living on the Oregon coast, with no family. When Jake mentioned the treasure hunt, both boys jumped at the chance for a family vacation and some adventure.

They all met in Chicago to spend a few days visiting the city sights before driving to the family farm in Harvard, Illinois. Jacob brought his wife and two boys and Ethan showed up with his girlfriend, Claire, an archeologist working for the state of Oregon. Molly liked her a lot and saw a great potential partner for her son . . . and she knew to keep her mouth shut and just talk to Jake about it. He would let her go on and on about how smart Claire was, how beautiful she was, how well-matched the two were. Then Jake would smile, give her a big hug, and say, "It's up to them, Mom. Let it be." She would hug him back and sigh.

The Beaucour clan piled into a large minibus and drove the two hours to Harvard. Molly had called the Morfords to let them know they were coming to visit, remembering the first time they went to the farm: Louise Morford met them with a shotgun, thinking they were religious or political fanatics; her husband,

Logan, came to their rescue and they enjoyed a wonderful visit with the couple.

Louise was so excited with their return visit she was telling all the neighbors about the Beaucours. When they pulled into the driveway, there were about a dozen folks waiting to meet them, all in a receiving line. As each Beaucour got off the bus, they would walk down the line, shaking hands and repeating their names. *Such friendly people*, Molly thought. She had prepared her grandsons for the country atmosphere and the strong accents. She warned them, "Meeting different people is always a big part of the adventure, and you always want to respect their customs and their language."

Louise and Logan were the last in the Morford line and they gave Molly and Jake big hugs. Molly introduced the rest of the family as they came down the line. Louise was so sweet to the grandchildren, giving them each a corncob pipe that she had carved herself. The boys were ecstatic, pretending to smoke their pipes all day long. Logan scooped up both boys and carried them to the pigsty, carefully leaning each one over the fence to pet the pigs. Squeals of laughter and plenty of comments about the smell. The boys loved it.

The neighbors bid farewell and left as the Beaucours and the Morfords went inside. While Jake took the family on a tour of the house, Molly helped Louise set out the luncheon. When everyone returned, they dug into the farmer's feast of fried chicken, ham, corn-on-the-cob, sweet peas, carrots, and mashed potatoes. Dessert was peach cobbler with lots of vanilla ice cream.

Logan explained how they raised the pigs and the chickens and planted their garden with the vegetables.

"You mean all this food came from this farm right here?" one of the boys asked.

"Yup, Louise and I plant the garden and take care of the animals. We go to the grocery store about once a month for some things, though mostly we eat what we raise."

"Wow," the other boy said. "We go to the store like every other day. We tried to have a garden once but if we depended on that we would all starve to death."

Jacob asked, "How is the farming business? I've heard about these corporation farms taking over. How do you feel about that?"

Logan discussed the farming industry with Jacob and Ethan while Molly and Jake told the boys about the horses. "Can we ride them?"

Louise patted them on the heads. "Well, of course you can. Have you little ones ever been on a horse before?"

"Yes, ma'am. We have riding lessons during the summer."

"Well, our big farm horses may be a bit much for you," Logan responded. "But if we walk on either side, I think you can make it."

"Could we walk up to the cemetery?" Ethan asked.

"That would be a perfect ride for the boys and a good walk to burn off some of this huge dinner," Logan said.

Everyone got ready while Logan and Jake got the horses. "No saddles, so I hope the little guys can ride bareback."

"I'm sure they'll be fine."

The farm horses stood twice as tall as the boys so Jacob and Ethan lifted them up onto the backs. "You hold onto these reins and squeeze with your legs." Jake and Ethan walked with one horse and Jacob and Logan walked with the other. The hike to the cemetery took about twenty minutes. The boys were so excited and proud.

"I'm going to be a cowboy when I grow up."

"Well, I'm going to be a farmer when I grow up."

The family reached the cemetery and helped the boys get off the horses. The boys proceeded to run through the graveyard hiding behind tombstones and playing tag. The adults wandered about reading the names of family members. They all met at François' grave.

"He married Marguerite after they left Québec," Molly told the story. "They used one of the gold bars to purchase this land and build the house and barn. Lived a nice farmer's life. We are still trying to figure out where the last gold bar ended up."

Ethan asked if it was okay to do a gravestone rubbing on the poster paper he had brought. Jake said, "Go right ahead. François would be happy to know his descendants still thought about him. Can you make copies for all of us? They would be nice keepsakes from our trip."

Ethan explained the process assuring everyone they would get copies. As the rubbing came through the paper, Claire studied it closely. "What a wonderful verse to sum up his life, *Do all the good you can, For as long as you can, For as many as you can, Until your end of days.*"

"Newspaper articles in the local library indicate that he lived that philosophy every day," Molly explained. "He mortgaged his house to pay for the local church, which is still standing, serving the community. He donated ten percent of his crop yield each year to a local charity to feed the poor. He hired several prisoners when they served their time and gave them a start on new careers. He seemed to care for others as much as he could.

"There was a funny phrase at the end of his will, kind of out of nowhere, scribbled in the margin," Molly explained. "It read: the treasure from the king is near his heart and even closer to his head. I wonder if the king's treasure is the gold bar? And if so, near his heart would be in the casket?"

Claire gasped. "Look at this! Molly!" Claire pointed to the gravestone rubbing. "Isn't this the French word for gold? And don't they call the bars ingots, *lingot d'or?*"

"What are you talking about?"

Claire spread Ethan's rubbing flat on the ground. "See this?" She outlined two words in the top corner of the gravestone: *lingot d'or.*

"Jake, look at this. Why would this be engraved on a tombstone? Oh, 'even closer to his head'. This has to have something to do with the bar."

Jake studied the tombstone. "Look at this. There's an arrow next to the words, pointing at the corner." He looked in the direction the arrow was pointing, trying to see a vault or some other place the bar might be hidden.

Ethan looked at the tombstone. He followed the arrow with his finger to the edge of the stone. "Dad, look here. See that groove. Why would you put that in a tombstone?"

Jake studied the groove and dug out his pocketknife. He carefully pressed the edge into the groove. Nothing happened. Jacob came to help.

"Dad, try it from different angles. If this is some kind of
door or secret compartment, there are many ways it could be put
together. Try it this way." Jacob pressed the knife again and a part
of the headstone moved slightly to one side.

Jacob gently pressed several more times and a piece of the
tombstone popped out of the corner. Something was wrapped in a
cloth inside the hole. Jake pulled it out. "This is pretty heavy for
such a small thing. Let's see." Jake unwrapped the cloth and a
shiny gold bar appeared. The family stood in awe.

"That's it!" Molly squealed. "The symbol of the king.
You've found it, near his head!"

"Molly, didn't you say that you found it strange that
François had purchased his own tombstone a year before his death?
You found that in his account ledger?"

"That's right, Jake. That's why he bought it, so he could
do this. But why not just give the gold bar to his son Jean? Why
hide it this way?"

"Well, Molly," Logan began. "I think I know the answer
and I beg your pardon, Jake, for sharing a family secret you may
not know." Everyone looked to Logan for an answer. "I always
wondered why your grandfather sold such a great farm to my
grandfather. Didn't make much sense selling something that grew
a lot of food for a lot of people and should be making lots of
money. So, when my daddy turned the farm over to me, I asked
him why Jean Beaucour sold the farm to us. He looked me sternly
in the eye, pointed his finger at my nose, and said, 'Don't you ever
get into gambling, young man. Jean Beaucour was a gambling
addict and he got so far in over his head, he had to sell the farm in
a rush. He didn't get half of what it was worth, but he got enough
to save his life, pay off his debts, and move far away from here.'
So, he sold the farm to get out of debt trouble."

"Which explains why my dad never got to be a farmer," Jake murmured. "By the time he was old enough, the farm was gone and he had to find a new career."

"As a lawyer," Molly continued. "Do you think François knew about the gambling?"

"I don't know about that," Logan replied, "but my guess is Jean would never have sold the farm if he had had that gold bar. And François probably wanted to protect it from his gambling habit, and so he hid the bar, hoping that someday someone would find his secret."

"Makes sense," Jacob concluded.

"Logan," Jake said. "This gold bar is on your land and so rightfully it belongs to you."

"No, no, no. That is in that tombstone and it belongs to the deceased and his family. That's not mine. To be honest, we got at least that much or more when Jean sold the farm to us for pennies on the dollar. I won't take that. It belongs to your family."

"You are a good person, Logan." Molly hugged him and he blushed.

Everyone walked or rode back to the farmhouse and enjoyed an afternoon snack of Louise's "wonderbars," similar to a granola bar, with a lot of chocolate all over it and a big scoop of homemade vanilla ice cream. After hugs and promises to visit again, the Beaucour clan climbed back into their minibus and headed for their Chicago hotel. Molly held her very heavy purse tightly.

Chapter 16

Mandragostan

Their arrival in Bulcan, Mandragostan, was very similar to the last time Gloria and Sophia had visited five years before. The airport was secure and bustling with business people. The roads were filled with traffic. People were moving about freely, even with the wreckage of war on many street corners. Gloria noticed armed women guards on several street corners, and security at the airport had been tight.

"They are really working hard to clean up this mess from the Bomani," Sophia said. "Look at the crews of workers clearing the streets and sidewalks." Bulldozers were scooping up the piles of rubble from explosions, and masons were patching holes in walls and giving buildings fresh coats of paint. Several of the main streets were normal but the side streets still showed the ravages of battle.

They passed the stadium surrounded by orange construction fences and troops. Heavy equipment was bringing loads of charred remains out to dump trucks. They learned later that no one was searching for any bodies or identifying any remains—the Bomani were unceremoniously disposed of in an old quarry outside of the city, their memory erased from the history of Mandragostan.

Schools were in session and children were enjoying the afternoon sun, playing in the schoolyards. Vendors were selling fruits and vegetables along the streets and a few tour buses were touring the city. It was clear that life was getting back to normal as quickly as the people could make it happen.

Their limousine pulled up to the large government building that Rabia had converted into her headquarters. The agents scanned for security noticing armed guards at the fortified gates, a series of jersey barriers controlling motorized vehicles entering the compound, security cameras, strategically placed clusters of troops prepared to engage any attack. A young woman smartly dressed in a business suit met them and escorted them to Rabia's offices. Rabia and her deputy jumped to their feet to greet the agents. They were in business attire, not military uniforms.

"It is so good to see you again, Gloria. Welcome, Sophia," Dalia said.

Rabia invited her guests to sit at the table as lunch was served. "First impressions?" Rabia asked.

"We will need to do an in-depth analysis but first impressions are very good. Dalia, you have planned the defense of this building very well."

"Thank you. Rabia and I have met with our strategic team daily to discuss multiple security problems around the city. We have a list of concerns." Dalia handed a sheet of paper to Sophia.

The four spent the afternoon reviewing the defenses of the building, which Rabia was now calling the Freedom Building. Then they covered the security around the utilities, water and electricity, and gasoline supply lines. There was a lengthy review of the security on the streets. Satisfied that the basic need of protecting the people was being met, Gloria moved on to the more difficult questions.

"You will remember the tiers of security," Gloria said, "focusing first on protection then sustainability. We will need to talk about your election process, which should be couched in a larger setting of the structure of the government. There are so many models of government, so you will need to formulate what you think the Mandragostan government should look like. For the past ten years, you have had a premier who was basically kept in power by the United States. If you are headed for a democratic approach with elections, you will need a government structure that reflects the power of the people's vote."

"We want the people to have a say in who rules their country and what the rules are. However, our people are not used to that kind of freedom, so they are easily swayed by whoever holds power. When the U.S was in charge, they followed their rules. When the Bomani invaded, they followed their rules. Now that we have taken control, they want to follow us. We need an interim period where we teach them about self-government and then try it."

"Dalia, do you have some people outside of Rabia's influence who you can trust?"

"I know several people who have not been a part of our army."

"Can you get a general sense of what the people think about Rabia as a leader? Like a survey of what people expect and want?"

"Well, everyone loves her. She is their savior."

"Okay, no offense to Rabia," Sophia said, "but Dalia, surely there are some people who don't want her to be in charge. Perhaps some who wanted the Bomani to stay in power."

Rabia sat quietly watching the process. Dalia looked toward Rabia. "Go ahead. I need you to be honest. Have you heard people speak out against us?"

Gloria could see that Dalia was choosing her words carefully. "First, the army is one hundred percent loyal. I have not heard anyone question any decision. They believe the cause of equality for women, children, and the elderly is critically important to our future. They see Rabia as their leader.

"Second, every woman I have spoken with in the city, with my uniform or without any identification, has praised Rabia for freeing them. There was one woman, the wife of one of the Bomani, who complained that her husband was gone, but then she said that was probably better for her since he couldn't beat her anymore. So, I think the women are behind Rabia, and that is almost sixty percent of our population.

"The group I worry about is the males. The elderly men will support her because she stopped the senseless beatings and forced labor. That's about ten percent. The young boys will not vote yet and that's another ten percent. But that leaves about twenty percent of the population, mostly men, who I just don't know about."

"Then one of our tasks is to find out if that twenty percent will support her ideas on self-government. With your permission, Sophia and I will disguise ourselves as men and circulate through the city listening to their ideas and viewpoints."

"As long as they don't catch you, that is brilliant," Dalia responded. "Just be very careful."

"Rabia, do you have any male advisers, any input from men at all?"

"No, not really," Rabia replied. "We have eliminated just about all the Bomani, many of whom were not even Mandragonian. The clerics with the Meglans cannot be trusted. Thus far, we are not executing them but they are pushing the limits with their constant demands to enslave women for their pleasure. We cannot let that continue much longer. The rest of the men are mostly merchants and laborers who just want to get back to normal life. I don't think they will care who is in charge as long as the economy is working."

"Great. Here's what I think we should do." Sophia and Gloria outlined a three-pronged program. "One, continue to search for any remaining Bomani men, cleaning out any they find. Two, infiltrate the Meglan clergy to find out what their plan is. Rabia may be able to get them on board with her ideas of freedom, or she may be forced to neutralize them. Three, meet with and enlist the merchants and laborers in the planning for the new government. They will be the pivot point to success."

They agreed to meet again in the morning to review and revise their next steps. After a light supper, Gloria and Sophia fell into bed, exhausted from their travels and the day's intense work. Before she went to bed, Gloria sent Rich an email outlining the day's events.

*   *   *   *   *

The agents were awakened shortly after midnight by an explosion and rapid gunfire. They were out of bed, armed and on the floor within seconds, ready for anything. The bursts of gunfire continued for about fifteen minutes and then silence fell on the compound. A speaker announced the assault had been dealt with and all were safe.

The next morning at breakfast, Dalia described the attack. Three men attacked the south gate, throwing bombs and grenades at the entrance. The guards responded by killing all three. At the same time a group of twelve assaulted the north wall. They tried to get over the wall and some also stormed the north gate. The four at the gate were killed quickly, and there were eight who were climbing the wall, crossing the razor wire, and attempting to drop into the compound. Only one made it over the razor wire and he died as he landed on the pavement. A security crew piled the bodies in the main square outside the Freedom Building for all to

see. At noon, there would be a public burning of the corpses.
Also, overnight, Rabia's troops had found three more clusters of
Bomani in the city and eliminated all of them.

Over breakfast Dalia and Rabia agreed to set up meetings
with the merchants and laborers. Dalia would set these up with a
high level of security. Sophia and Gloria explained how they
would infiltrate the clerics. The tasks for the next few days would
help in establishing a new government.

The input from the merchants and workers strongly
supported any government that would promote a healthy economic
environment and bring tourism to Mandragostan. Dalia organized
a council of businessmen to discuss ways to improve the image of
the country and invite tourists to their nation. The merchants were
pleased they had been invited to share their thoughts. These
meetings began a very positive relationship within the city.

Rabia invited five prominent Mandragonian lawyers, three
women and two men, to meet with her to discuss the planned form
of government and elections. All five favored a system based on a
constitution that established three branches of the government.
While similar to the United States, they agreed the government
must be smaller and simplified. Since most Mandragonians lived
in the capital, the focus was on organizing the city into regions or
districts while also providing ways for the rural population to have
representation. They knew it would take several weeks of
meetings to organize the details but agreed on a six-month interim
government led by Rabia and her military group, elections, and
then another six-month transition to the elected representatives,
president, and courts. The rural areas would form two districts and
the city would form six districts.

Sophia and Gloria had a much more eye-opening
experience dressed as men and attending cleric meetings with the
Meglans. Their cover story included disguises that were so
convincing they were able to use the men's restrooms without any

questions. They posed as clerics from one of the rural towns, stating to the group that they firmly believed in the Meglan mission and would fight to the death to support them. This opened up the discussion within the group and the clerics shared their plans. They were very clear that they supported the Bomani's position on women, the elderly, and children. Females were slaves that existed for men's pleasure and to bear offspring. They were beasts of burden and should do housework only. Women should not be educated.

The elderly were a curse on the nation and any elder person who could not carry his or her own weight was useless and should be killed. The Meglans wanted every person over the age of sixty to be registered and forced to work. All boys needed to be indoctrinated in Meglan religious schools for boys, and girls should be institutionalized to understand their place in the home. Girls needed to learn how to serve and boys needed to learn how to dominate. The clerics did not want Western tourists who were bad influences on the people, and they wanted all technology controlled and limited to only the cleric society. Gloria and Sophia wanted to shoot them all right then. They were patient and played their roles.

Gloria cleverly led them on, asking how the rural clerics could support them. The clerics outlined a plan to overthrow Rabia's army by poisoning their water supply. As her army fell sick and died, she would be powerless to fight the clerics who would easily take over the government and establish a new order. Sophia secretly recorded all the meetings so that Rabia's people could hear the treachery being planned. After three hours of meetings, the two agents thanked the clerics for their guidance and pledged to return to the countryside and raise funds and find men to support their cause. They returned to Rabia's offices.

*   *   *   *   *

Dalia's troops had captured one of the Bomani that assaulted the Freedom Building and interrogated him. At first, he refused to cooperate but the women were brutal in their interviewing techniques. When they threatened to remove the soldier's privates, he gave in and broodingly told them everything he knew. The most important part of the information was his allegiance to the clerics and the identity of the leader of their assault team, a member of the Meglan religion.

As the information from the interrogation came to Rabia's table, Sophia and Gloria's report on the clerics brought the situation into focus. It was clear that the Meglans were a direct threat to the future of the country.

After four weeks of intense work, Rabia thanked the two agents for their help and support and asked them to leave Mandragostan. "You should not be here as we address this threat. You can honestly report to anyone who asks you that you have no idea what we are planning to do. Over the next three months I will invite historians and political scientists to help us write a constitution. I will state to the people that I will rule for one year as the interim leader and then I will step down when the election is complete. We will contact Pristine International to establish a fair and secure voting process. Your guidance has helped us greatly but you must not be a part of the actions necessary to achieve it. If your government asks, you don't know what will happen."

Gloria and Sophia hugged Rabia and Dalia wishing them good luck with their plans. "You know you can count on us for anything. Don't hesitate to contact us."

Chapter 17

Sweden

Sophia and Gloria kept Rich and Jen posted each day on their activities in Mandragostan. When they informed the Crocketts that Rabia had asked them to leave, there were a series of questions to find out why. While the two agents had their suspicions about what Rabia was planning, they could honestly respond that they did not know what would happen next. Jen and Rich were relieved that Rabia did not expect Veritas to help her set up the new government. The company could honestly answer the persistent questions from the State and the Defense departments with "We don't know."

Sophia asked if they could visit Hilda Berkheimer for a few days in Sweden on an annual security check-up visit. It had been six weeks since the confrontation with Noah in the Bahamas and the two agents needed a break. Jen said that was a great idea and to enjoy Sweden. "Watch out for that Swedish vodka. It packs a real punch."

The next morning Gloria and Sophia were on the company jet flying to Sweden. A company car took them to Smalander Castle in Strangnas. The Berkheimers had purchased the castle in 1992 and completely renovated the Victorian-era structure. The estate included a thousand acres of virgin forest and a ten thousand square foot mansion built from granite, a grand home including a ballroom, several sitting rooms, and ten bedrooms. The house was surrounded by a raised terrace with imposing grand staircases in the front and back. There was a vast lawn and a formal garden at the back of the house. The lawn was the size of two football fields and carefully manicured. The formal gardens stretched along each side of the lawn where large oak and fir trees loomed overhead to provide shade. The entire estate was enclosed within a ten-foot-high fortified stone wall.

The renovated mansion was a modern, up-to-date domicile enclosed in an 18th Century shell. Maureen had added a large gazebo at the far end of the lawn. She insisted they build a safe room under the gazebo with a tunnel extending from the main house to the gazebo. The Berkheimers were Veritas clients and each year an agent would visit Smalander to review and update security, the job of Gloria and Sophia this year.

Hilda Berkheimer, a beautiful blonde with blue eyes and a short, very athletic body, was well known throughout Sweden as a loving and kind mother to her children, a shrewd businesswoman in her professional relationships, and a social asset and intellectual equal to her husband, Conrad. Her children's books were an international success. She was also a close friend of Molly.

Gloria and Sophia had met Hilda during a recent, harrowing adventure in Iceland. Trapped in an underground prison for several hours, the three had shared secrets from their past lives. They had developed a special bond during those hours of impending doom before discovering a way to escape. Sophia felt a few days in Sweden with Hilda would help Gloria get over her encounter with Noah.

Conrad and Hilda greeted the agents at the front staircase. Conrad was leaving for a busy afternoon at Olafson Associates, his conglomerate of companies developing renewable energy sources. Conrad Berkheimer was well known across the world for his innovative thinking on creating new forms of energy.

"So good to see you both. We're looking forward to the grand opening of the Italian Villa hotel. Hope to see you there. Enjoy your day with Hilda and I will see you for dinner." Conrad slid into the limousine and was whisked away.

"Come on in, girls. I understand we have some things to talk about."

Hilda led the agents into one of the sunny sitting rooms overlooking the formal gardens. A maid served brunch as they sat down.

"I've forgotten what a beautiful garden you have," Gloria said. "This must be a calm and heartwarming place to recover from the turmoil in the world."

"It is. I've lived here in Sweden now for almost fifty years. Conrad and I renovated this castle in 1992 and raised four children here. It is always a comfort to come home after book tours and charitable events. Conrad is still going strong at work for a man in his seventies, much like Jake."

Hilda briefly reviewed her history from her days as Molly's best friend, Maureen, to her assignment in the FBI organized crime division, to her move to London to hide from the mob, and her escape to Sweden. "Much like you, Gloria, my old identity died in the English Channel, and my rebirth was a complete change of life. It is still amazing to me that after all these years Molly was able to find me. Unfortunately, the mob had one of their goons looking for me, too, and this is where we cleaned that up. You can't see any of the damage but he died in that gazebo. Thank goodness for my two close assistants who cleaned up everything. Other than Molly, Jake, Rich, and Jen and of course you two, no one knows. Conrad still doesn't know about that awful day."

"I think it is more amazing that you have been able to hide this for so many years from Conrad. It must have been horrible to have a battle like that in your own home."

"This secret will follow me to my grave. My legacy will be my four children and my books of Swedish fairy tales. Maureen died long ago and remains buried.

"So, Sophia, how is married life treating you? Any family plans yet?"

Sophia blushed. "We are working things out really well. We spend every weekend in Boston or Bryn Mawr, and we FaceTime all week. No family plans, yet."

"Ha, but if you saw some of that FaceTime you would think she would get pregnant online," Gloria joked. Sophia poked Gloria in the arm.

Hilda smiled and chuckled. "Enjoy every minute of it. My time with Conrad has been the best. Live, love, and laugh."

"Well, at least I don't have to live a second life. Petr knows about my years with that awful Francesca de la Rondo and the deal I cut with the police to put her in prison. Growing up running with the neighboring Italian boys, having to defend myself as they got older, I decided to join the military. My goal was to become a commanding officer in the Italian Special Forces; unfortunately, I was assigned to protect the president of Italy who gave me away to de la Rondo like I was his personal property. I worked for her at first because I was commanded to but then the violence grew on me and I turned my skills to promoting her empire.

"I was sent to Egypt to kill Carol Hook, but lucky for me, Jake Beaucour knew how to shoot an arrow. That three-thousand-year-old Egyptian arrow really stung, but it made me realize just how screwed up I had become. Thank God for Jake. And as for FaceTime, you better not be sneaking a peek, you computer geek!" Sophia laughed as Gloria raised her eyebrows.

"Your privacy is safe with me." Gloria crossed her heart.

"And how about you, Gloria? I understand there may be something going on with Noah Chambers?"

It was Gloria's turn to blush. "You two found your true loves without any baggage attached. I stumbled upon Noah and I knew he had a lot of dirty laundry. In my previous life, I used him as a fence and he doesn't even realize who I am. I think Veritas has done a great job of reinventing me.

"But I have to give him credit. He admitted to his criminal life and he described it as an addiction that he can't give up. I love him very much but I simply cannot be with him if he is going to be crooked. Such a difficult dilemma." Gloria talked about their business deal ten years before and her sudden realization at the wedding that they had met in Paris. She said she had never felt this way about any man, although she was absolutely determined to stay on the straight path that Molly and Jake had given her.

"Oh my," Hilda said. "You've got it bad. I can tell by the way you talk about Noah that you are in love. And I also know how hard you have worked to leave Rachel behind. My advice would be to tell him the truth about you."

"But the problem I see with that is he could use it to blackmail me, and I'm not sure I can trust him. Maybe if things work out, eventually, but for now I'm sticking with Gloria Lovelace."

"I see your point. How about an afternoon in Stockholm, ladies? Check out the ice bar and some of the great shopping?"

They enjoyed a wonderful afternoon in town, returning to Smalander for dinner with Conrad. He was always so much fun to be with, full of stories about the "good old days" and sharing his newest ideas on improving energy sources. Dinner was a delicious repast of Swedish dishes ending with the national drink, Kronan Swedish Punsch, a blend of rich rums poured over ice with a squeeze of lime.

Sophia and Gloria enjoyed Hilda's hospitality for two more days. The visits to town, the shopping, lunches out, and afternoon siestas were a welcome relief. The agents decided it was time to return to Veritas the next morning.

Hilda hosted a dinner with several of her close neighbors attending to wish Fire and Ice a healthy new year and a safe trip home. The evening was filled with many stories and wonderful Swedish foods, and of course the customary Kronan. As the conversation drifted from one topic to another, Gloria's phone notified her of a text message.

"Excuse me, I have to check on this text." Gloria moved to the sitting room. She opened the text, from an unknown cellphone number. The cryptic message caught her by surprise.

Gloria-I really need your help. Please, please respond. Love Noah.

*   *   *   *   *

Fire and Ice left Smalander the next morning. As they drove out the gate, Conrad turned to Hilda with questioning eyes.

"Oh Conrad, you know these love affairs and all their secrets. Gloria is in the throes of deciding if this young man Noah is worth her trouble."

"Secrets? Gloria has secrets?"

"Don't we all, Conrad?"

"Oh, do we?"

"Conrad, I have something to tell you about my life before I met you."

"Oh, my darling," Conrad interjected with a loving mist in his eyes, "I've always known you had a 'different' life before we met. And I've always loved 'this you' with all my being. You are my Hilda forever, regardless." So sweetly was it said that she actually felt weak in the knees.

EPILOGUE

Bryn Mawr

"Any word from Sophia and Gloria?"

"No," Jake replied. "Fire and Ice are officially visiting clients in Hawai'i. Unofficially, they are searching for Noah to see why he needs help. They'll be there for two weeks and Petr will join them during the second."

"Lucky them, Hawai'i. That's pretty nice."

"We have our own trip to plan, dear. Jane and Elena have completed the Italian villa renovation and are opening their next boutique hotel near La Spezia on the Northern coast of Italy. Can't wait to return to that area. Those cute little seaside towns and the beautiful beaches."

"And those cute little bikinis." Molly poked Jake in the ribs.

"Now, Miss Molly, I only need one girl in a bikini, and her pool is right here." Jake motioned out the window to the backyard.

"Let's check that out, Mr. Beaucour."

Author's Notes

In light of the current situation in the world, the country of Mandragostan is a creation for the purpose of this story. The turmoil in this setting mirrors many of the trouble spots around the world today, though it is not intended to focus on any actual country or particular group of radicals. The focus of the story is on women establishing their independence in a region that subjugates them.

Mandragostan is an imaginary setting in the Rwenzori Mountains of Central Africa, south of the Sahara Desert, near Uganda, South Sudan, and Rwanda, and is inhabited by poor families trying to survive in an agrarian lifestyle where pockets of good farming land are very productive.

The Bomani (Egyptian for "warriors") are a fictional terrorist group of twenty thousand who believe it is their destiny to rule the world. Women, children, and the elderly are beneath them and exist only to serve their needs. The leader rules by ruthless brutality and those challenging him are brutally killed. The followers are loyal to him and will do anything for their promised positions of power. Conquering the whole world, one country at a time is the primary goal of the Bomani.

Moseley's Landing in the Virginia Beach area is fictitious, though William Moseley was an authentic immigrant to the shores of the Elizabeth River in Virginia in 1648.

www.ingramcontent.com/pod-product-compliance
Lightning Source LLC
Chambersburg PA
CBHW071322130726
47996CB00002B/590